致敬译界巨匠许渊冲先生

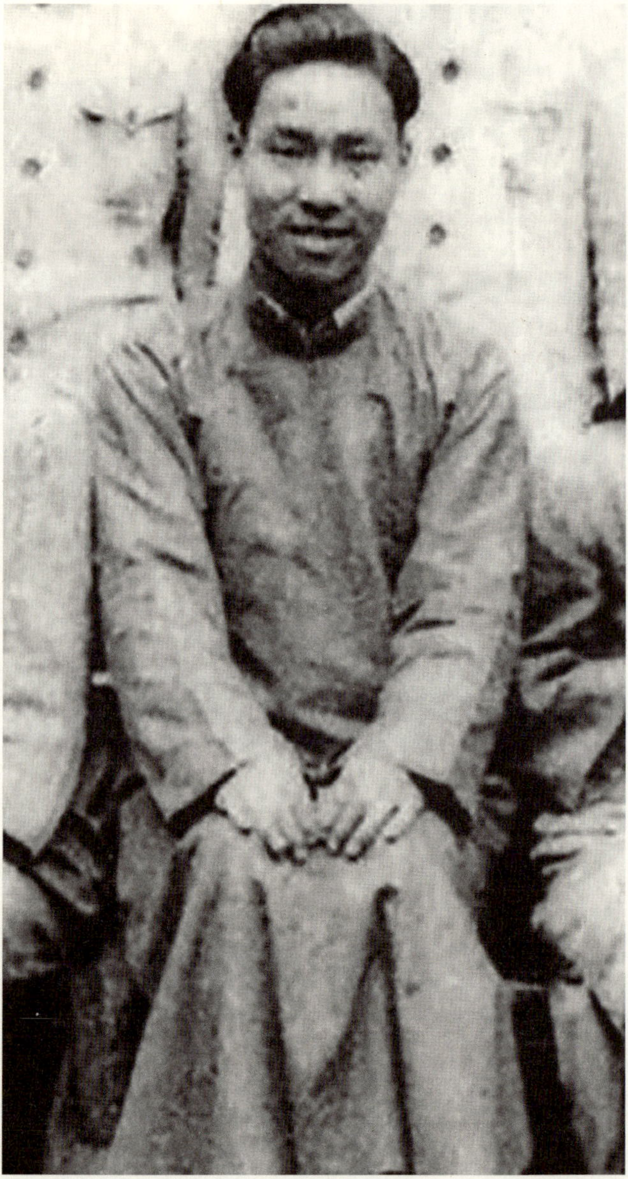

许 渊 冲 译
陶 渊 明 诗 选

SELECTED POEMS OF TAO YUANMING

| 编 | 译 |

中国出版集团
中译出版社

目录 Contents

| 译序

002 时运（四首其一）
Spring Excursion (I)

004 时运（四首其二）
Spring Excursion (II)

006 时运（四首其三）
Spring Excursion (III)

008 时运（四首其四）
Spring Excursion (IV)

010 停云（四首其一）
Hanging Clouds (I)

012 停云（四首其二）
Hanging Clouds (II)

014 停云（四首其三）
Hanging Clouds (III)

016 停云（四首其四）
Hanging Clouds (IV)

018 庚戌岁九月中于西田获早稻
Early Crop in the West Field

022 癸卯岁始春怀古田舍（二首其二）
Farmwork (II)

024 游斜川
A Trip to the Slanting Stream

026 怨诗楚调示庞主簿邓治中
A Southern Complaint

028 答庞参军
Reply to Pang

030 五月旦作和戴主簿
Written on the 1st Day of the 5th Moon in the Same Rhymes as Secretary Dai

032 和刘柴桑
In Reply to Liu Chaisang

034 酬刘柴桑
Reply to Liu, Prefect of Chaisang

036 和郭主簿（二首其一）
In Reply to Secretary Guo (I. Summer)

038 和郭主簿（二首其二）
In Reply to Secretary Guo (II. Autumn)

040 癸卯岁十二月中作与从弟敬远
For My Cousin Jingyuan

042 始作镇军参军经曲阿作
On My River Journey

044 乙巳岁三月为建威参军使都经钱溪
Qian Stream Revisited

046 归去来兮辞
Home-Going-and-Coming Song

054 形影神（三首其一：形赠影）
Body, Shadow and Spirit (Body to Shadow)

056 形影神（三首其二：影答形）
Body, Shadow and Spirit (Shadow to Body)

058 形影神（三首其三：神释）
Body, Shadow and Spirit (Spirit)

062 九日闲居
Written at Leisure on Double Ninth Day

064 归园田居（五首其一）
Return to Nature (I)

066　归园田居（五首其二）
　　Return to Nature (II)

068　归园田居（五首其三）
　　Return to Nature (III)

070　归园田居（五首其四）
　　Return to Nature (IV)

072　归园田居（五首其五）
　　Return to Nature (V)

074　乞食
　　Begging for Food

076　连雨独饮
　　Drinking Alone on Rainy Nights

078　移居（二首其一）
　　Moving House (I)

080　戊申岁六月中遇火
　　My Cottage Caught Fire in Midsummer

084　饮酒（二十首其一）
　　Wine-drinking Song (I)

086　饮酒（二十首其四）
　　Wine-drinking Song (IV)

088　饮酒（二十首其五）
　　Wine-drinking Song (V)

090　饮酒（二十首其七）
　　Wine-drinking Song (VII)

092　饮酒（二十首其八）
　　Wine-drinking Song (VIII)

094　饮酒（二十首其九）
　　Wine-drinking Song (IX)

096 饮酒（二十首其十）
Wine-drinking Song (X)

098 饮酒（二十首其十一）
Wine-drinking Song (XI)

100 饮酒（二十首其十三）
Wine-drinking Song (XIII)

102 饮酒（二十首其十四）
Wine-drinking Song (XIV)

104 饮酒（二十首其十六）
Wine-drinking Song (XVI)

106 饮酒（二十首其十七）
Wine-drinking Song (XVI)

108 饮酒（二十首其十九）
Wine-drinking Song (XIX)

110 饮酒（二十首其二十）
Wine-drinking Song (XX)

112 止酒
Abstinence

114 责子
Blaming Sons

116 拟古（九首其三）
Old Styled Verse (III)

118 拟古（九首其四）
Old Styled Verse (IV)

120 拟古（九首其七）
Old Styled Verse (VII)

122 拟古（九首其九）
Old Styled Verse (IX)

124 杂诗（八首其一）
Miscellaneous Poems (I)

126 杂诗（八首其二）
Miscellaneous Poems (II)

128 杂诗（八首其三）
Miscellaneous Poems (III)

130 杂诗（八首其四）
Miscellaneous Poems (IV)

132 杂诗（八首其五）
Miscellaneous Poems (V)

134 杂诗（八首其六）
Miscellaneous Poems (VI)

136 杂诗（八首其七）
Miscellaneous Poems (VII)

138 杂诗（八首其八）
Miscellaneous Poems (VIII)

140 咏贫士（七首其一）
A Poor Scholar (I)

142 读《山海经》（十三首其一）
Reading *The Book of Mountains and Seas* (I)

144 拟挽歌辞（三首其一）
An Elegy for Myself (I)

译序

王安石说"陶诗有奇绝不可及之语",如"心远地自偏"超越人境,所以能闹中见静;"悠悠见南山"融情于景,所以能与山共鸣;"飞鸟相与还"爱山及鸟,所以能投入自然;"此中有真意"不足为外人道也,结果是天人合一。《时运》一诗"称心""易足",更是与古人同乐了。

《菲华文艺》第26卷第4期刊登了符家钦的《我爱陶潜饮酒诗》《古今奇绝话陶诗》,文中介绍了施颖洲和我的英译,文后附的施颖洲注认为:施、许"译法大体上相似,但亦稍有不同""许教授有时避重就轻,爱惜思力"。施译用抑扬四音步译五言诗,许译用五音步。施译一韵到底,许译共押五韵。施译"模仿原诗语气、文体。许译有时用反语,或加解释"。我看,比较一下施译和许译,对提高译诗的质量,也许不无好处。

符家钦在文中引用王安石的话说:"陶诗有奇绝不可及之语,如'结庐在人境,而无车马喧。问君何能尔?心远地自偏'四句,自有诗人以来无此句。"这四句诗为什么"奇绝不可及"呢?因为诗人在"车如流水马如龙"的客观环境里,居然听不见"车马喧"。这就说明诗人的主观修养已经超越了客观环境,能够闹中见静了。下面我们看看针对"而无车马喧"

一句,施和许的译文:

施译: No noise of coach or horse sounds here.
许译: There's noise of wheels and hoofs, but I hear not.

比较一下两种译文,可以说施译的"无车马喧",译得"字字精确"。许译把"车"译成 wheels(车轮),把"马"译成 hoofs(马蹄),这是不是"避重就轻,爱惜思力"呢?我的看法是:车轮、马蹄更重动态,施译相形之下,反倒更重静态。所以我不是"避重就轻",反倒是避易就难,再"思"而译的。这句诗最重要的是个"无"字,"无"有两种解释:一是客观上真没有"车马喧",一是主观上听不见"车马喧"。施译强调客观,许译强调主观。如果是前者,那么下一句"问君何能尔"的意思就是:问你怎么可能在"人境"而没有"车马喧"呢?这个"能"字指客观的可能性。如果是后者,那意思是:问你怎能听不见"车马喧"呢?"能"字指"君"的主观能力。到底是指主观还是指客观?还要再看下一句:"心远地自偏"。如果"地自偏"指客观环境偏僻,那没有"车马喧"和"心远"有什么关系呢?心在远方或不在远方,偏僻的地方不是一样没有"车马喧"吗?如果是指主观,那意思是:只要你心高意远,即使是"车马喧"的"人境",也会"自"然而然变得像"偏"僻的"地"方一样了。现在再看看施和许对这句的翻译:

施译: The mind's remote, the earth'll be bare.
许译: Secluded heart creates secluded place.

施译强调客观,说心在远方,地上自然没有"车马喧"。

许译强调主观，说心静地自静。到底哪种译法更接近这四句"奇绝不可及之语"呢？

陶诗第五六句"采菊东篱下，悠然见南山"是全诗名句。如果说"心远地自偏"写诗人的主观思想超越了客观环境，那这两句却写诗人和"南山"共鸣，一样"悠然"，超越了主观自我，达到了忘我境界，忘了个人的祸福成败，与南山同生死，进入了人与自然合而为一的最高境界，所以这两句诗传诵千古。陶诗七、八句"山气日夕佳，飞鸟相与还"写诗人不但思想上与"南山"一致，情感上也与"飞鸟"一致，与鸟同乐，也达到了"天人合一"的境界。最后两句"此中有真意，欲辨已忘言"在我看来，所谓"真意"，是指人应静如南山，动如飞鸟，指诗人所向往的游乐于天地自然之道而忘怀人世的境界。这六句，施译和许译"大体上相似"。"真意"二字，施译是 true sense，更加形似；许译是 revelation（启示），更加神似。不同之处是：施译"一韵到底"，更加音似；许译共押五韵，更重音美。这里我要指出：施译 here 和 clear 是一韵，bare、there 和 pair 又是一韵，不能算是"一韵到底"，其实是每隔 16 个音节才有一韵的。陶诗原文每隔 10 字一韵，许诗也是每隔 10 个音节一韵，用韵密度反比施译更加接近原文。总之，施译更重微观意似、音似、形似，许译更重宏观意美、音美、形美。

现将这首《饮酒》诗的施译和许译抄录于后，以便比较。

施译：

I built my hut in peopled world,

No noise of coach or horse sounds here.

You ask me how could it be so?

The mind's remote, the earth'll be bare.
Chrysanthemums picked by east hedge,
I see at ease the south hills there.
The mountain air's fair day and night.
The flying birds come home in pair.
In all these things there is true sense,
I lose the words to make it clear.

许译：

Among the haunts of men I build my cot;
There's noise of wheels and hoofs, but I hear not.
How can it leave upon my mind no trace?
Secluded heart creates secluded place.
I pick fenceside chrysanthemums at will
And leisurely I see the southern hill,
Where mountain air is fresh both day and night,
And where I find home-going birds in flight.
What is the revelation at this view?
Words fail me even if I try to tell you.

比较一下施译和许译，我看施用四音步译五言诗，更加精练，于是也把译文改成八音节：

In people's haunt I build my cot,
Of wheel's and hoof's noise I hear not.
How can it leave on me no trace?
Secluded heart makes secluded place.

I pick chrysanthemums at will,
Carefree, I see the Southern Hill.
The mountain air is fresh day and night,
Together birds go home in flight.
What revelation at this view?
Words fail me if I try to tell you.

"心远地自偏"原来用了一个动词 makes，那就多了一个音节；如果把 secluded 改成 seclud'd，那又破坏了抑扬格的节奏；最后就把动词删了。

《中国翻译》1995 年第 4 期第 17 页上说："翻译方法学不应由一系列的规范组成，而应该描述翻译者能够采用而且已经采用过的一切可能的策略。"现在，我要谈谈国内外译者已经采用的陶渊明的诗《时运》英译的方法。译文分别选自 20 世纪 70 年代美国印第安纳大学出版社出版的《葵晔集》，80 年代中国香港商务印书馆出版的《陶渊明诗文选译》，90 年代北京大学出版社出的《汉魏六朝诗》。下面是《时运》第一段原文、语体译文[*]和三种英译：

迈迈时运，	天回地转，时光迈进，
穆穆良朝。	温煦的季节已经来临。
袭我春服，	穿上我春天的服装，
薄言东郊。	去啊，去到东郊踏青。
山涤余霭，	山峦间余剩的烟云已被涤荡，
宇暧微霄。	天宇中还剩一抹淡淡的云。

* 语体译文选自《陶渊明集全译》，贵州人民出版社，1996 年。

有风自南,　　　清风从南方吹来,
翼彼新苗。　　　一片新绿起伏不停。

译文 1

By and by, the seasons come and go,

My, my! What a fine morning!

I put on my spring cloak,

And set out east for the outskirts.

Mountains are cleansed by lingering clouds;

Sky is veiled by fine mist.

A wind comes up from the south,

Winging over the new sprouts.

——《葵晔集》,印第安纳大学出版社

译文 2

Rolling, rolling, nature moves in its course,

Mildly, mildly smiles this fair day.

I put on my garment of the season,

And go eastwards to greet the spring.

The hills emerge from the dispersing clouds,

While a thin mist hangs over the horizon.

Up from the south a wind is risen

To skim over the fresh fields of green.

——《陶渊明诗文选译》,香港商务印书馆

译文 3

Seasons pass by,

Smiles this fine day.
In spring dress, I
Go eastward way.
Peaks steeped in cloud.
In mist veiled spring.
South wind flaps loud
O'er sprouts like wing.

——《汉魏六朝诗》，北京大学出版社

陶诗叠字很不好译，第一、二句"迈迈""穆穆"，译文1用了by and by 和my, my，前者重复by，可以说是形似，后者重复my，可以说是音似；译文2重复了rolling和mildly，可以说是意似；译文3没用叠字，从词的观点来看，既不形似，也不音似，只用一个by传达"迈迈"之意，只用一个smile传达"穆穆"之情，也许可以算是神似。第三句的"春服"，译文1、译文3都用spring，可以算是直译；译文2却用season，可以算是意译。第四句的"东郊"，译文1最为形似；译文2、译文3都只译"东"而不译"郊"，译文2并且加了to greet the spring（迎春），更能传达原诗的意美，这也是译"春服"二字没有直译，而用意译的原因（为了避免重复spring）。第五句的动词"涤"字很形象化，译文1用了cleanse（洗净），可以说是正译；译文2用了emerge（涌现，尤其是从水中涌现），那就是把云比作水，而从水中涌现不是洗涤了吗？所以译文2可以算是反译，也就是从反面说；译文3用了steep，本义是"浸沉"，引申义是"笼罩"，用在这里，本义和引申义都合适，可以算直译兼意译。第六句的"暖"字，译文1、译文3都用veil（盖上面纱),比译文 2 更形象化。第七句"有风自南"的动词,译文 1 用 come,译文 2 用 rise,都不如译文 3 的 flap(拍拍翅膀)形象化。第七句原文并没有形象化的字眼,译文 3 是不是不符合原诗风格呢?从句的观点来看也许不符合,但联系第八句的"翼"字来看,译文 3 和译文 1 可以说都胜过了译文 2。由此可见,可以从字、词、句、段几个不同的角度来评论。如果微观和宏观有矛盾,一般说来,可以为宏观而牺牲一点微观,也就是舍卒保车。

现在再看陶诗《时运》第二段的原文、语体译文和三种英译:

洋洋平津,	长河已被春水涨满,
乃漱乃濯。	漱漱口,再把脚手冲洗一番。
邈邈遐景,	眺望远处的风景,
载欣载瞩。	看啊看,心中充满了喜欢。
称心而言,	人但求称心就好,
人亦易足。	心满意足并不困难。
挥兹一觞,	喝干那一杯美酒,
陶然自乐。	自得其乐,陶然复陶然。

译文 1

Bank to bank, the stream is wide;

I rinse, then douse myself.

Scene by scene, the distant landscape;

I am happy as I look out.

People have a saying:

"A heart at peace is easy to please."

So I brandish this cup.

Happy to be by myself.

——《葵晔集》，印第安纳大学出版社

译文2

Wide and deep the leveling fords;

I rinse my mouth, I wash my feet.

Lovely in the haze the distant scene.

With glee I smile, with joy I gaze.

As the common saying runs:

Self-content brings us peace of mind.

Thus I quaff off my cup of wine,

To find myself dunk with delight.

——《陶渊明诗文选译》，香港商务印书馆

译文3

In wide lake green

I steep my knee.

On happy scene

I gaze with glee.

As people say,

Content brings ease.

With wine I stay

Drunk as I please.

——《汉魏六朝诗》，北京大学出版社

第二段第一句"洋洋平津"，"津"是河、渡头的意思，也有说是"平泽"意思的,那就是湖了。译文1是河,译文2是渡头,译文3是湖。"洋洋"二字,译文1重复bank,说两岸之间河流宽阔。以词而论,"洋洋"和bank并不意似,重复只是形似;以句而论,译文1却是意似。译文没有重复"洋洋",这是有所失,但重复了bank(河岸),这是有所创,也就是说"失之东隅,收之桑榆","以创补失"了。译文2把"洋洋"译成wide and deep(宽而深),以词而论,比译文1更意似;但没有叠词,又不如译文1形似。译文2把"津"译为渡头,渡头一般比较浅,译文说"宽而深",那又不够意似了。第二句"乃漱乃濯",重复"乃"字,句子平衡。译文2加词则译成漱口洗脚,既意似,又形似,胜过译文1。译文3减词,没译漱口,不如译文2;但把"濯"字译成"浸到膝盖",似乎更能传达暮春水滨洗濯、祓除不祥的意思。第三、四句原文和第一、二句对称,译文1重复scene,只是形似而不意似;译文2第四句句内对称,句外又和第二句译文对称,既意似,又形似,可以说是远远胜过译文1和译文3。第五、六句可能是全诗中心思想,译文2似乎比译文1更能传达原诗"知足常乐"的内容,而译文3却更精练。如果说第五、六句是抽象的理论,那么第七、八句饮酒自得其乐就是具体的事实,三种译文各有千秋。由此可见,以句而论,有些译文可见高低,有些却是难分上下。

下面再看陶诗《时运》第三段的原文、语体译文和三种英译:

延目中流,	放眼望河中滔滔的水流,
悠想清沂。	遥想古时清澈的沂水之湄,
童冠齐业,	有那十几位课业完毕的莘莘学子

闲咏以归。	唱着歌儿修禊而归。
我爱其静,	我欣羡那种恬静的生活,
寤寐交挥。	清醒时,睡梦里时刻萦回。
但恨殊世,	遗憾啊!已隔了好多世代,
邈不可追。	先贤的足迹无法追随。

译文 1

Peering into the depths of the stream,

I remember the pure waters of the Yi,

There students and scholars worked together,

And, carefree, went home singing.

I love their inner peace,

Awake or asleep, I'd change places,

But, alas, those times are gone—

We can no longer bing them back.

——《葵晔集》,印第安纳大学出版社

译文 2

I direct my eyes to the midstream,

And think of the waters of the limpid Yi,

Where once gathered many a goodly youth,

Singing freely on their homeward way.

I love their easy tenor of life;

Walking or asleep the scene comes to me.

O how I regret to be born much belated,

And the light of other days ever receding!

——《陶渊明诗文选译》,香港商务印书馆

译文 3

I gaze mid-stream
And miss the sages
Singing their dream
Of Golden Ages.
How I adore
Their quiet day!
Their time's no more
And gone for aye.

——《汉魏六朝诗》，北京大学出版社

第三段包含了一个典故。《论语》中说："莫春者，春服既成，冠者五六人，童子六七人，浴乎沂，风乎舞雩，咏而归。"译成语体就是：暮春三月，春天衣服都穿定了，我同五六个成年人、六七个青年，在沂水旁边洗洗澡，在舞雩台上吹吹风，一路唱歌，一路回来。诗中的"清沂""童冠""咏归"都指《论语》中的故事。译文 1 的译者可能不知道这个典故，所以第三句"童冠齐业"译成 worked（工作），这和原意恰恰相反，第六句译文也有问题，可以算是误译。译文 2 是直译，但对不知道典故的读者来说，还是读不出春游之乐。译文 3 联系第四段第七句的"黄唐莫逮"(赶不上黄帝和唐尧的盛世，即黄金时代），这才不但传达了原诗的言内之意，还传达了言外之意。由此可见，从字、词、句、段的观点来看，译文 3 仿佛都不似原文，但从全诗的观点来看，译文 3 却比译文 1 和译文 2 都更能传达原诗之美。

最后，我们看看《时运》第四段的原文、语体译文和三种英译：

斯晨斯夕，	这样的早晨，这样的夜晚，
言息其庐。	我止息在这简朴的草庐。
花药分列，	院子里一边药栏，一边花圃，
林竹翳如。	竹林的清荫遮住了庭院。
清琴横床，	横放在琴架上的是素琴一张，
浊酒半壶。	那旁边还置放着浊酒半壶。
黄唐莫逮，	只是啊，终究赶不上黄唐盛世，
慨独在余！	我深深地感慨自己的孤独！

译文 1

In the morning and at night
I rest in my house.
Flowers and herbs are all in place;
Trees and bamboos cast their shadows.
A clear-sounding lute lies on my bed,
And there's half a jug of coarse wine.
Huang and Tang are gone forever;
Sad and alone, here I am.

——《葵晔集》，印第安纳大学出版社

译文 2

This morn, and also this night,
A quiet heart within a quiet cot.
I see the flowers and herbs, row by row,
And the trees and bamboos, thick and shady.
The pure-toned zither before my knee,

And half a pot of unstrained wine.
Then my fancy roves to the age of gold.
But O, why am I left here all alone.

——《陶渊明诗文选译》，香港商务印书馆

译文 3
In light or gloom,
I rest at ease
'Mid grass and bloom,
Bamboos and trees,
A lute on bed,
A jug of wine.
Golden age's fled;
Alone I pine.

——《汉魏六朝诗》，北京大学出版社

第四段第一句"斯晨斯夕"重复了"斯"字，译文 1 没有重复，只是意似而不形似；译文 2 不但重复 this，而且在第二句重复了 quiet（静），说是庐静心地静，是创造性的翻译；译文 3 则把"晨夕"改为"晨昏"（白日黄昏），可以算是意译。原文第三、四句对称，译文 1 不如译文 2，译文 2 用的是加词法，译文 3 用的是减词法。第五、六句原文还是对称，译文 1、译文 2 都不如译文 3 形似，译文 3 读来，简直有点像《怒湃集》(*Rubaiyat*) 第十二首。第七句"黄唐"指黄帝、唐尧，译文 1 音似而不意似，远远不如译文 2 和译文 3 的"黄金时代"（意译）。

比较一下三种英译文，基本上可以说译文 1 是直译，译文2是意译，译文3是韵译。从词的观点来看，直译可能更接近原文，更符合原文用词的风格；从句的观点来看，意译更接近原文，更符合原文造句的风格；从全诗的观点来看，韵译更接近原诗，更符合原诗有韵律的风格。原诗每句四字，译文1和译文2却每行字数多少不一，只有译文3每行四个音节，更能传达原诗的形美。原诗每两句押一韵，译文1和译文2都不押韵，只有译文3隔行用韵，更能传达原诗的音美。至于意美，以词而论，译文3可能不如译文1；以句而论，译文3可能不如译文2；但以全诗而论，译文3却又胜过译文1和译文2。总之，从意美、音美、形美的"三美"观点来看，我觉得韵译比直译、意译更能使人知之、好之、乐之。如从对等原则来看，可能直译比意译和韵译更对等，更符合原文的风格。但我认为，原则来自实践，如果符合对等原则的译文不如符合"三美"原则的译文能使人知之、好之、乐之，那应该修改的是对等原则，而不应该把"三美"的译文改成"对等"。

许渊冲译陶渊明诗选

时 运

（四首其一）

迈迈时运，穆穆良朝。

袭①我春服，薄②言③东郊。

山涤余霭，宇暧④微霄。

有风自南，翼⑤彼新苗。

① 袭：衣上加衣，即从一件衣服上再套一件衣服。

② 薄：到。

③ 言：语气助词无实意。

④ 暧(ài)：遮挡，遮蔽。

⑤ 翼：名词用作动词。写南风吹拂春苗的样子就像张开的翅膀。

公元404年，40岁的陶渊明，正闲居在家乡寻阳柴桑（今江西九江）。他在3月3日（古代三月三有修禊的风俗）出游东郊，想起曾点说过的一番话，写下了这首记游的组诗——《时运》。

开头"迈迈""穆穆"两个叠词，声调悠长，"迈迈"形容时间一步一步地推进；"穆穆"形容春色温和宁静；似乎整个时空和诗人的意绪有着同样的韵律。"春服出东郊"写出诗人悠然自得、随心适意的情怀。后四句写郊外所见景色：山峰涤除了最后一点云雾，露出清朗秀丽的面貌；天宇轻笼着一层若有若无的淡淡云气，显得格外高远缥缈；南风吹拂春苗，禾苗欢欣鼓舞，像鸟儿掀动着翅膀。这些写景的句子从简朴中显出精巧，看似漫不经心，却恰到好处。同时这广大、明朗、平和、欢欣的邈远的画面，又是诗人精神世界的象征。

Spring Excursion

(I)

Seasons pass by,
Smiles this fine day.
In spring dress,
I go eastward way.
Peaks steeped in cloud,
In mist veiled spring.
South wind flaps loud,
O'er sprouts like wing.

时 运

（四首其二）

洋洋平泽，乃①漱乃濯②。
邈邈遐景，载欣载③瞩。
称④心而言，人亦易足。
挥⑤兹一觞⑥，陶然⑦自乐。

① 乃：连词，表示衔接。
② 濯（zhuó）：洗。
③ 载……载……：古文中用来表示同时进行的两个动作。
④ 称：符合，适合，与……相适应。
⑤ 挥：举起。
⑥ 觞（shāng）：酒。
⑦ 陶然：喜悦、快乐的样子。

    "洋洋平泽"是指水势浩大而湖面平坦，诗人就在这湖里洗涤；"邈邈遐景"是指远处的景色辽阔而迷蒙，充满了吸引力，令诗人欣喜。洋洋的水面和邈邈的远景融为一体，似乎和自然化成了一个整体。暗指多数人违背人的自然本性而产生缺损和痛苦，从中表达人应遵循自然规律。"人亦易足"指人生原本是容易满足的，诗人由此景而产生人生感悟：人但求称心就好，心意满足并不困难。举起酒杯一饮而尽，在蒙眬中自得其乐。

Spring Excursion

(II)

In wide lake green,

I steep my knee.

On happy scene,

I gaze with glee.

As people say,

Content brings ease.

With wine I stay,

Drunk as I please.

时 运

(四首其三)

延目中流,悠悠清沂①。
童冠②齐业,闲咏以归。
我爱其静,寤寐交挥。
但恨殊世,邈③不可追。

① 沂(yí):河名,出水于山东东南部。

② 童冠:童子与冠者,即未成年者与年满二十者。古代男子二十行加冠礼,表示已成年。

③ 邈(miǎo):远。

"延目中流"是指诗人将目光投注到湖中水波上。遥想古时清澈的沂水之湄,以及《论语·先进》中曾皙所描绘的一幅图景:有一群习完课业的学生,悠闲地唱着歌回家。言外之意,诗人向往这样平静悠闲的生活。"我爱其静,寤寐交挥。"不论日夜都向往诗中所描绘的平静悠闲的生活,说明"静"是诗人所处的世界中最为缺乏的。"邈不可追"指先贤的足迹无法追随。遗憾与自己的时候相去遥远,无法追及,因此从遥想回到现实中。

Spring Excursion

(III)

I gaze mid-stream
And miss the sages
Singing their dream
Of Golden Ages.
How I adore
Their quiet day!
Their time's no more
And gone for aye.

时 运

（四首其四）

斯晨斯夕，言息其庐。

花药分列，林竹翳如。

清琴横床，浊酒半壶。

黄①唐莫逮②，慨独在余。

① 黄：黄帝。唐：唐尧。两者是中国历史上贤明的君主领袖。

② 逮：赶得上。

  此章是诗人春游后回到居所所叙。"斯晨斯夕，言息其庐。"指这样的早晨，这样的夜晚，我止息在这样简朴的草庐。诗人回到平时生活的家中，入眼的是庭园景色和室内陈设，小径两旁的花卉药草，以及交相掩映的绿树青竹；横放在琴架上的素琴，旁边半壶浊酒。清楚地显现出院内清静的气氛和主人清高孤傲的情怀。最后一句因未能追赶黄唐盛世而感慨自己的孤独。诗人追求的人格，是真诚冲和、不喜不惧；所追求的社会，是各得其所、怡然自乐。

Spring Excursion

(IV)

In light or gloom,

I rest at ease

'Mid grass and bloom,

Bamboos and trees,

A lute on bed,

A jar of wine.

Golden Age's fled,

Alone I pine.

停 云

停云，思亲友也。
罇①湛②新醪，园列初荣③，
愿言不从④，叹息弥襟。

(四首其一)

① 罇(zūn)：同"樽"，酒杯的意思。
② 湛(zhàn)：深。引申为盛满。
③ 初荣：刚开的花。
④ 从：顺从，满足。

霭霭停云，濛濛时雨。
八表⑤同昏，平路⑥伊⑦阻。
静寄⑧东轩，春醪⑨独抚⑩。
良朋悠邈，搔首⑪延伫⑫。

⑤ 八表：八方，泛指天地之间。
⑥ 平路：平地。
⑦ 伊：语气助词。
⑧ 寄：住在。
⑨ 醪(láo)：醇厚的酒。
⑩ 抚：拿着，举着。
⑪ 搔首：挠头，指焦急等待的样子。
⑫ 延伫：长时间站立等待着。

公元404年春，当时作者闲居于家乡浔阳柴桑（今江西九江）。此诗为思念亲友而作。开篇直叙：酒樽里盛满了澄清的新酒，后园内排列着初绽的鲜花，可是我美好的愿望不能实现，叹息无奈，忧愁充满我的胸怀。

"霭霭停云，濛濛时雨。"指阴云在空中凝聚不散，春雨绵绵意迷蒙。"八表同昏"等诗句，表面上看是写天气，形容春季的天色，实则因国政时局被封建贵族、军阀争夺中央政权而搞得天昏地暗，暗喻诗人关怀世难的忧心。诗人以景衬情，此情此景尽显寂寞，春时新酿之醪却也只有自己品尝，因此思念好友之情更甚。

Hanging Clouds

The Hanging Clouds reveals my longing for my kinsfolk and my friends. My jar brimming with newly brewed wine and my garden overgrown with flowers, my longing for my folk cannot be satisfied. So it bursts into sighs.

(I)

Heavy the hanging cloud,

Misty the drizzling rain.

With darkness overflowed

The sky and earth remain.

Mute in east room I stay;

Alone I drink spring wine.

For my friends far away,

I scratch my hair and pine.

停 云

（四首其二）

停云霭霭，时雨濛濛。

八表同昏，平陆成江。

有酒有酒，闲饮东窗。

愿言①怀②人，舟车靡③从。

① 愿言：思念急切深重的样子。

② 怀：思念。

③ 靡（mǐ）：不能。

    良朋好友在远方，翘首久候心落空及舟车不通亦难相见。该首运用比兴的手法和复沓的章法，通过对自然环境的烘托描写和不能与好友饮酒畅谈的感慨，充分说明了诗人对好友的深切思念之情。

Hanging Clouds

(II)

Heavy the cloud is hanging,
Misty the rain is drizzling.
Land into water changing,
The sky and earth are grizzling.
Let me drink wine on wine
By east window at leisure:
How much for friends I pine!
But they can't come with pleasure.

停 云
（四首其三）

东园之树，枝条载①荣②。
竞用新好，以怡余情③。
人亦有言，日月于征④。
安得⑤促席，说彼平生。

① 载：开始。
② 荣：植物繁茂的样子。
③ 竞用新好，以怡余情：春树竞相用美好的景色使我心情愉悦。竞：竞争。新好：春天的树。
④ 征：行，这里指时间流逝。日、月：时间。
⑤ 安得：怎么能得到。

"竞用新好，以怡余情。"说的是春树春花展新姿，使我神情顿时清朗。诗人对友人的一片热忱和一往情深，使得诗人陷入寂寞孤独。也正是因寂寞孤独而生幻觉。想起平日听人们所说的能与好友促膝长谈，共诉平生情意长。实在是羡慕飞落庭前树梢上悠闲鸣唱的鸟儿。怎奈思念良朋不得见，无可奈何而越发"抱恨"了。

Hanging Clouds

(III)

The eastern garden trees
Burst with green leaves again;
In new attire they please
My heart with might and main.
It is said time and tide,
Sun and moon wait for none.
Could we talk side by side
About what we have done?

停 云
（四首其四）

翩翩飞鸟，息我庭柯①。
敛翮②闲止③，好声④相和。
岂无他人？念子⑤实多。
愿言不获，抱恨如何⑥！

① 柯：树枝。
② 翮(hé)：鸟的翅膀。
③ 止：停留。
④ 好声：悦耳的声音。
⑤ 子：这里指朋友。
⑥ 如何：怎么办，无可奈何。

《停云》全篇贯穿了诗人因不能和友人共享美好时光的抱恨之意，充分表现了诗人对友人的一片热肠和希望与友人共享美好时光的深情。

Hanging Clouds

(IV)

No longer on the wing,
Birds rest on garden trees.
They flutter and then sing
In harmony to please.
Have I no other friend?
It's you I can't forget.
I can't attain my end.
How can I not regret?

庚戌岁九月中于西田获早稻

人生归有道①,衣食固②其端③。
孰是都不营?而以求自安④。
开春理常业⑤,岁功聊⑥可观。
晨出肆⑦微勤,日入负⑧耒还。
山中饶⑨霜露,风气亦先寒。
田家岂不苦?弗获⑩辞此难⑪。

① 道:规律,道理。
② 固:本来。
③ 端:第一,首要的。
④ 孰是都不营?而以求自安:如果弃之不经营,自己如何能心安?孰:如果。是:这,此,这里指衣服和食物。
⑤ 常业:农活。
⑥ 聊:勉强,尚且可以。
⑦ 肆:操作,干活。
⑧ 负:扛着,背着。
⑨ 饶:富饶、多的意思。
⑩ 获:能够。
⑪ 此难:这种艰难,这里指农耕生活。

公元410年九月,陶渊明46岁,这是他弃官彭泽令归田躬耕的第6年。在这年秋收后,他以郑重又愉快的心情创作了这首诗。

起笔两句,把传统文化中的"道",与衣食并举,意义极不寻常。衣食的来源,本是农业生产。"孰是都不营,而以求自安?"诗人认为,人生应以生产劳动、自营衣食为根本。

Early Crop in the West Field

Of life there is a proper way:
Provide your food from day to day!
If you don't do work of such kind,
How can you set at ease your mind?
If I work as usual in spring,
I know then what this year will bring.
At sunrise I do labor light;
I come back with my crop at night.
Frost will fall early in the hill,
So you can feel the evening chill.
Don't peasants know their life is hard?
But they can't leave their humble yard.

四体诚①乃疲，庶②无异患③干④。
盥濯息檐下，斗酒散襟颜。
遥遥沮溺⑤心，千载乃相关。
但愿长如此，躬⑥耕非所叹。

① 诚：的确。
② 庶：大体上。
③ 异患：想不到的祸灾。
④ 干：侵犯。
⑤ 沮溺：即长沮和桀溺，孔子遇到的"耦而耕"的隐者。这里指隐士。
⑥ 躬：亲自。

若为了获得衣食俸禄，而失去独立自由之人格，就宁肯弃官归田。"开春理常业，岁功聊可观。"言语似乎很平淡，但体味起来，其中蕴含着真实、淳厚的欣慰之情。"田家岂不苦？弗获辞此难。"稼穑愈是艰难辛苦，愈见诗人躬耕意志之深沉坚定。"襟颜"指胸襟和面颜；诗人是在为自由的生活、为劳动的成果而开心。诗人不仅是一位农民，还是一位传统文化所造就的士人。他像一位农民那样站在自家屋檐下把酒开怀，可是他的心灵却飞越千载，尚友古人。结笔说："但愿长如此，躬耕非所叹。"但愿长久地过这种生活，自食其力，自由自在，纵然躬耕辛苦，也无所怨尤。

诗人的心灵，经过深沉的省思，终归于圆融宁静。意志坚如金石。引发其对人生真谛的思考与总结。

Tired will grow their four members old.
But there's no evil unforetold.
After washing their hands and feet,
Under the eaves they drink wine sweet.
The hermits living long ago,
Shared with us the same weal and woe.
I will live so under the sky;
Over farmwork I'll never sigh.

癸卯岁始春怀古田舍

(二首其二)

先师①有遗训,忧道不忧贫。
瞻望②邈③难逮④,转欲志长勤⑤。
秉⑥耒⑦欢时务⑧,解颜⑨劝农人。
平畴⑩交远风,良苗亦怀新⑪。
虽未量晨功,即事多所欣。
耕种有时息,行者无问津⑫。
日入相与归,壶浆劳近邻。
长吟掩柴门,聊⑬为陇亩民⑭。

① 先师:孔子。
② 瞻望:敬仰。
③ 邈:遥远。
④ 逮(dài):企及,赶得上。
⑤ 长勤:长期劳动。
⑥ 秉:持,手里拿着。
⑦ 耒(lěi):犁柄,泛指农具。
⑧ 时务:及时应该做的事情,这里指农耕。
⑨ 解颜:面带笑容。
⑩ 畴(chóu):田野。
⑪ 怀新:麦苗生机勃勃。
⑫ 津:渡口,这里引申为长沮、桀溺的事,即归隐田园从事农耕。
⑬ 聊:姑且,尚且。
⑭ 陇亩民:田野之人,即农民。

该首为公元403年春所作。公元402年,进占荆州的桓玄又进一步攻陷京师,称太尉,总揽朝政。国事无望,使诗人坚定了躬耕自资的决心,并付诸实际行动。这首诗便是陶渊明亲自参加春耕之后的作品。"忧道不忧贫"诗人怀念先师孔子遗训,体悟其中不易,从而深感忧道之人的难得。暗指诗人想成为长沮、桀溺那样的隐士。"虽未量岁功,既事多所欣。"这一年的粮食并未进行估算,劳作就已经使我很开心,表达诗人劳作的喜悦之情。字里行间仍透露着对世道的关心和对清平盛世的向往。最后一句又归隐田园之中,昭示了一种"极高明而道中庸"的人生境界。

Farmwork

(II)

Confucius told us to do properly
And not to worry about poverty.
How to follow our Master who sees far?
I can be busy as all farmers are.
In time I will do farm work, plough in hand,
Smiling, I talk with them who till the land.
Winds coming from afar caress the plain;
Tender shoots welcome spring to come again.
Though we know not how much we'll reap this year,
Yet farm work in the field evokes our cheer.
At times when we are tired, we take a rest,
None come to inquire about east or west.
Coming back when the sun's on the decline,
I'll see my neighbors with a pot of wine.
Crooning a poem, then I close the door.
Content, what does a farmer need for more.

游斜川

开岁倏五日，吾生行①归休。
念之动中怀②，及辰③为兹游。
气和天惟澄，班坐④依远流。
弱湍驰文纺⑤，闲谷矫⑥鸣鸥。
迥泽⑦散游目⑧，缅然⑨睇⑩曾丘⑪。
虽微⑫九重⑬秀，顾瞻无匹俦⑭。
提壶接宾侣，引满更⑮献酬⑯。
未知从今去，当复如此不？
中觞纵遥情，忘彼千载忧⑰。
且极⑱今朝乐，明日非所求。

① 行：即将，将要。
② 动中怀：内心激动。
③ 及辰：及时，趁着这个好日子。及，赶得上。
④ 班坐：按次序列坐。
⑤ 文纺（fǎng）：有花纹的鲂鱼。文，通"纹"。
⑥ 矫：高飞。
⑦ 迥泽：宽阔的湖水。迥，广远，宽阔，广阔。
⑧ 散游目：向远处看，随意观赏。
⑨ 缅（miǎn）然：认真思考的样子。
⑩ 睇（dì）：斜着看，凝视。
⑪ 曾丘：即曾城。
⑫ 微：无，比不上。
⑬ 九重：指昆仑山的曾城九重。
⑭ 匹俦：匹敌，比得上。
⑮ 更：更替，轮流。
⑯ 献酬：互相劝酒。
⑰ 千载忧：指对生死的忧虑。出自《古诗十九首》之十五："生年不满百，常怀千岁忧。"
⑱ 极：尽兴。

公元414年，陶渊明50岁。正月初五，"天气澄和，风物闲美"，他和两三邻里，偕游斜川，不禁欣慨交心，悲喜集怀。故作此诗。"开岁倏五日"说的是新年匆匆又过去了五日，年过半百的诗人感慨时光飞逝，离生命休止的时候亦不远了，尽显诗人悲伤之感。胸中不免有些激荡，于是趁此良辰携朋友春游。诗人用较华丽的笔墨着意写出游的鱼、飞的鸟都是那么的怡然自得，水底、空中无处不洋溢着生机，体现着诗人的欣喜和向往。湖水深广，层丘高耸，构成佳境，令人神驰意远，凝视曾城沉思良久。美景宜人便提起酒壶款待游伴，不禁将此情此感吐露出来。此时诗人有些伤感如此欢乐今后能否依旧。酒喝到微醉放开豪情便全然忘却了忧愁，最后以"且极今朝乐，明日非所求"展现诗人旷达的胸怀及超脱的人生观。

A Trip to the Slanting Stream

Five days of the new year have passed;
My life is drawing near the last.
Can I not free my heart from sorrow?
We make this trip before tomorrow.
Steeped in fresh air and bright sunbeam,
We sit along the rippling stream.
In sparkling waves breams swim with pleasure;
In quiet vales gulls scream at leisure.
The brimming lake arrests the eye;
I muse on the pagoda high.
Though not so high as the Ninth Tier,
It commands a view without peer.
I pass the jar of wine around,
And ask friends in wine to be drowned.
I know not if another day
We can enjoy still in this way.
Half drunk, we may blow hot or cold,
Forgetting the sorrow age-old.
If we can enjoy our fill but now,
Oh, let tomorrow knit its brow!

怨诗楚调①示庞主簿邓治中

① 怨诗楚调：即《楚调曲》中的《怨诗行》，载册于汉乐府《相和歌》。庞主簿，庞遵，诗人的朋友，主簿是其官职，主管朝廷簿书。邓治中，其姓名不详，治中是其官职，负责诸曹文书的管理，也是诗人的朋友。

天道幽且远，鬼神茫昧然。
结发②念善事，僶俛③六九年④。
弱冠⑤逢世阻，始室⑥丧其偏。
炎火屡焚如，螟蜮⑦恣⑧中田。
风雨纵横至，收敛不盈廛⑨。
夏日长抱饥，寒夜无被眠。
造⑩夕思鸡鸣，及晨愿乌⑪迁。
在己何怨天，离忧凄目前。
吁嗟身后名，于我若浮烟。
慷慨独悲歌，钟期⑫信⑬为贤。

② 结发：束发，指十五岁。借指青年时期。
③ 僶(mǐn)俛(miǎn)：勤奋努力。
④ 六九年：五十四岁。
⑤ 弱冠：二十岁。
⑥ 始室：三十岁。
⑦ 螟(míng)蜮(yù)：祸害庄稼的害虫。
⑧ 恣(zì)：肆意迫害。
⑨ 廛(chán)：古时候一户人家所占用的土地。不盈廛：收获的粮食不多。
⑩ 造：到了。
⑪ 乌：指太阳。相传日中有三足乌，故称太阳为金乌。
⑫ 钟期：即钟子期，春秋时期楚国人，是伯牙的朋友。《列子·汤问》："伯牙鼓琴，志在高山，钟子期曰：'峨峨然若泰山'；志在流水，曰：'洋洋然若江河'。子期死，伯牙绝弦，以无知音者。"这里用以指庞主簿、邓治中，意思是说他们一定也能像钟子期那样体会到这"悲歌"的含义。
⑬ 信：的确。

公元418年，陶渊明54岁，仿照《楚调曲》中《怨诗》的体裁写给自己朋友的一首诗。作品分前后两段，前段14句，诗人从自己半生的艰难遭遇出发，对自古以来众口所说的天道鬼神的存在提出了怀疑。"天道幽且远"指天道冥冥莫测，玄奥深远，暗指鬼神之事渺茫难知。以此开头作为结论，贯穿全段。"弱冠逢世阻"说的是20岁身处乱世，历尽艰难险阻。指明遭遇的开始。天灾人祸，庄稼无收、挨饿受冻，已经陷入绝境。"在己何怨天"说的是这怪自己怨不得天，变相地表现他对当时政治的不平。"慷慨独悲歌，钟期信为贤。"说的是忧情激荡，独自悲伤歌咏，钟子期那样的知音，定会为我感叹！表现了陶渊明在这种极其痛苦难熬的生活中的意志坚定，宁死不屈，如此气节在精神道德上获得了胜利的骄傲与自豪。

A Southern Complaint

The way to Heaven's dim and far,
Who knows what gods and spirits are.
At fifteen I learned to do good,
At fifty-four I passed manhood.
While young, I went a rugged way;
My lute-string broke before its day.
The burning sun scorched my fields;
The insects damaged my corn yields.
The wind and rain raged up and down;
I could not reap half I have sown.
Hunger stared me at summer's height;
Cold bed freezed me in winter night.
At dusk I waited for cocks to crow,
At dawn for the sun to sink low.
Not Heaven but I am to blame;
What e'er I do, I'm still the same.
What matters the fame after death?
It will vanish like smoke or breath.
Alone I pour out plaintive song.
Will connoisseurs listen for long?

答庞参军[1]

[1] 参军：汉末设立的古代官职，负责参谋军务。

相知何必旧？倾盖[2]定[3]前言。
有客赏我趣，每每顾林园。
谈谐无俗调，所说[4]圣人篇。
或[5]有数斗酒，闲饮自欢然。
我实幽居士，无复东西[6]缘。
物新人惟旧，弱毫[7]多所宣[8]。
情通万里外，形迹滞江山。
君其爱体素，来会在何年？

[2] 倾盖：车盖，形状像伞。
[3] 定：证实，证明。
[4] 说：通"悦"，喜欢。
[5] 或：有时。
[6] 东西：为求职做官而东西奔走。
[7] 弱毫：指毛笔。
[8] 宣：表达，指写信。

公元424年，陶渊明60岁。庞参军在浔阳为官，与陶渊明遂成"邻曲"，后庞参军奉命出使江陵，有诗赠陶渊明以告别，陶渊明以此诗作答。此诗分两部分，前八句追忆与庞参军真挚深厚的友情，后8句抒发依依惜别的情怀。

"相知何必旧"指相互知心的人未必是旧相识，说明两人不是旧交，而是新知。"赏我趣"指欣赏我的志趣。此乃谦虚的说法，同时也说明了独特的人格、高雅生活的魅力。"圣人篇"说明两人谈话内容格调不俗气，皆先圣遗篇；"闲饮自欢然"指悠闲对饮心自欢然，说明诗人的交友方式高雅、闲适，感情流露自然、融洽，亦有舒适欢喜之感。"但愿先生保重贵体，将来相会知在何年？"诗人与好友分手在即，不免感伤、怅惘；感伤之余，亦有嘱咐。更对来年的重新相会寄托了希望。体现了诗人与朋友之间真挚的友情。

Reply to Pang

Friends may not be acquaintances old,

Chance meeting may warm winter cold.

If we enjoy the same delight,

Your visit beautifies the site.

We talk unlike the vulgar kind,

The sage will elevate our mind.

When we have a jar of good wine,

Home brew would become drink divine.

A lonely hermit fond of rest,

I go no longer east or west.

All men love new things and friends old.

Let news in black and white be told.

Though severed by mountains and streams,

We're joined in the heart shedding beams.

You love a rural life, but when,

In which year can we meet again?

五月旦作和戴主簿

虚舟纵逸棹,回复遂无穷。
发岁①始俯仰②,星纪③奄④将中⑤。
南窗罕悴⑥物,北林荣且丰。
神萍⑦写⑧时雨,晨色奏⑨景风⑩。
既来孰不去?人理固有终。
居常待其尽,曲肱⑪岂伤冲⑫?
迁化或夷险,肆志无窊⑬隆。
即事如已高,何必升华嵩?

① 发岁:开岁,一年的开头。
② 俯仰:形容时间短暂。
③ 星纪:古代星岁纪年法中十二星次之一。此处指癸丑年。
④ 奄:通"淹",忽然、突然的意思。
⑤ 将中:将要到年中,指五月。
⑥ 悴:憔悴,这里是枯萎的意思,指干枯的植物。
⑦ 神萍:神话中的雨师,主管人间的降雨。一作"萍光",一作"神渊"。
⑧ 写:同"泻",下大雨的意思。
⑨ 奏:通"凑",聚集,凝结。
⑩ 景风:古代指祥和的风。
⑪ 曲肱(gōng):即"曲肱而枕之",就是把胳膊弯曲当做枕头。
⑫ 冲:空虚,淡泊名利,这里指道的最高境界。
⑬ 窊(wā):指低处的坑洼。

此诗写于公元413年,陶渊明49岁。诗人从时光的流逝、季节的循环往复和景物的荣衰更替,而体悟到人生有始亦必有终的道理。

"虚舟纵逸棹"说的是轻舟上飞快地划着船桨,暗指时光流逝日月如梭。接着写五月时的自然万物:南窗和北林的花草树木都生机盎然;雨神及时降下甘雨,清晨吹拂和暖的南风。"既来孰不去?"说的是人既生来谁能不死?诗人在这里明知故问,揭示自然规律,有来必有去;人生亦如此,有生必有死。指引人们坦然地面对,安心地生活。体现出诗人的人生观,心灵是自由的。"即事如以高"指倘若能对眼前事物达观视之,又何必访仙祈求长生。意指诗人归隐之后的决心,及怡然自得的人生态度。

Written on the 1st Day of the 5th Moon in the Same Rhymes as Secretary Dai

Time flies like an empty boat with swift oar;
Four seasons circulate and reappear.
Looking back, the New Year's Day is no more;
Now we come near the middle of the year.
By southern window there're no withered trees;
In northern grove we find leaves lush and green.
Morning seems beautified by summer breeze,
And timely rain washes the country clean.
Who comes on earth shall go, such is our fate,
And what begins will end, such is our life.
Though changeless, for the changeful we may wait;
Content with poverty won't lead to strife.
Our life is full of weal and woe,
On ups and downs our mind can't rest.
If we don't care for what is high or low,
Why should we climb to mountain crest?

和刘柴桑

山泽久见招,胡事乃踌躇?
直为亲旧故,未忍言索居①。
良辰入奇怀,挈杖还西庐。
荒途②无归人,时时见废墟。
茅茨③已就治,新畴④复应畬。
谷风转凄薄,春醪解饥劬⑤。
弱女⑥虽非男⑦,慰情良胜无。
栖栖⑧世中事,岁月共相疏。
耕织称其用,过⑨此奚所须?
去去⑩百年外⑪,身名同翳如⑫。

① 索居:独自生活在一个地方。
② 途:道路。
③ 茅茨(cí):茅草屋。《诗经·小雅·甫田》:"如茨如梁。"茨:屋盖。已就治:已经修补整理好。就,成功。
④ 新畴:新开垦出来的田地。
⑤ 劬(qú):疲乏,劳累。
⑥ 弱女:古代人家生了女孩就开始酿酒,随即就埋藏在山坡上,等到出嫁的时候再挖出来饮用。这里借指为薄酒。
⑦ 男:与之相对应,是醇酒的意思。
⑧ 栖栖:忙碌不安的样子。
⑨ 过:超过,除……以外。
⑩ 去去:不断地逝去,指时间的流逝。
⑪ 百年外:人死后。
⑫ 翳(yì)如:湮灭,暗淡。

公元409年,陶渊明45岁。此诗是陶渊明为回答刘柴桑邀请他隐居庐山而作。这是一首和诗,诗人闲话家常,回答友人刘遗民的问题,并对其表示安慰和劝勉之意。

开篇乃兴来之笔,以新创一问一答形式。"良辰入奇怀"指良辰美景入胸怀。"入"还与下句形成鲜明的方向感,暗指诗人未忘怀现实的衰败。"茅茨已就治,新畴复应畬"说的是简陋的茅屋已修葺,还需治理新垦田,指明诗人未忘却世事,在力所能及的范围内做着本分的事——传授门生。"栖栖世中事,岁月共相疏"说的是世间之事多忙碌,岁月已使人们彼此越来越远,是极好的警世之句。

In Reply to Liu Chaisang

Hills and lakes attract me for long.
Should I stay away from their song?
It's for my kinsmen near and dear
That nowhere else I would appear.
Fine morning enters curious breast,
Cane in hand, I head for Cot West.
Along the way no passers-by
But ruined huts arrest the eye.
I have repaired my thatched cot
And plough new furrows in my plot.
When valley wind turns chill at first,
I drink spring wine to quench my thirst.
A daughter cannot help as man
But she will comfort as she can.
The court affairs seem far away
From us with each year and each day.
I plough and weave enough for me;
From other needs I am carefree.
A hundred years will come to end,
Then life and fame with death will blend.

酬刘柴桑

穷居寡人用，时忘四运周。
门庭多落叶，慨然已知秋。
新葵郁北牖①，嘉穟②养南畴。
今我不为乐，知有来岁不？
命室携童弱③，良日登远游。

① 牖（yǒu）：墙上的窗子。
② 穟（suì）：饱满的禾苗。
③ 童弱：子侄等，泛指孩子。

公元 414 年，陶渊明 50 岁。这年秋天，刘柴桑下庐山来拜访陶渊明，相互作诗和唱，陶渊明于是作下《酬刘柴桑》。

"穷居寡人用，时忘四运周"说的是居住在偏僻的地方甚少与人交往，有时竟忘记了一年四季的轮回变化，暗指诗人在感受知与不知的生命意趣。"今我不为乐，知有来岁不？"说的是如今我要及时享受快乐，因为不知道自己明年是否还在世上，暗指生命的荣盛将不再。"命室携童弱，良日登远游"说的是吩咐妻子带上孩子们，趁着美好的时光一道去登高远游，充分体现诗人的洒脱。

Reply to Liu, Prefect of Chaisang

Living unsociable behind closed gate,
I care not how four seasons circulate.
When I see fallen leaves along the way,
I sigh for the coming of autumn day.
Gloomy marrows at northern wall vibrate,
And paddy fields in the south undulate.
If I do not enjoy delight, then how
Can I know next year as happy as now?
So I tell wife and children to go out
To climb a hill or wander thereabout.

和郭主簿

（二首其一）

蔼蔼堂前林，中夏贮清阴。
凯风①因②时来，回飙开我襟。
息交③游闲业，卧起④弄书琴。
园蔬有余滋，旧谷犹储今。
营己良有极，过足非所钦⑤。
春⑥秫⑦作美酒，酒熟吾自斟。
弱子戏我侧，学语未成音。
此事真复乐，聊用忘华簪⑧。
遥遥望白云，怀古一何⑨深！

① 凯风：南风。
② 因：遵循，按照。
③ 息交：停止官场的交流活动。
④ 卧起：夜间和白天，即一整天。
⑤ 钦：美慕。
⑥ 春（chōng）：捣掉谷类的壳皮。
⑦ 秫（shú）：粘高粱。两者多用来酿酒。
⑧ 华簪（zān）：贵重的发簪，这里比喻做官。
⑨ 一何：多么。

公元408年，陶渊明44岁。这是他归家两年后所作。这组诗描写了夏日乡居的淳朴、悠闲的生活，表现出摆脱官场牢笼之后那种轻松自得、怀安知足的乐趣。

该首写景色。"蔼蔼堂前林"说的是堂前林木茂盛。仲夏时节，在浓厚的树荫下乘凉，南风不时吹来，尽显诗人悠闲舒适之态，可谓乡村景物之乐。在这期间，读书弹琴，起卧自由，为精神生活之乐；蔬菜有余，存粮犹储，乃诗人对物质知足之乐；自斟自酌，是癖好满足之乐；与妻儿团聚，小儿膝下承欢，真乃天伦之乐。以上数乐，让世人忘却官场腐败，世风伪诈，享受其隐逸恬淡之乐。尽显诗人坦率胸襟，淳朴情境真挚动人，表达了诗人安贫乐道、恬淡自甘的心境。

In Reply to Secretary Guo

(I. Summer)

The shady trees before my hall
Store coolness against summer heat.
The south wind comes at season's call,
My lapel welcomes its breath sweet.
Not sociable even at leisure,
I rise to play my lute or read.
Eating my garden greens with pleasure,
I've stored up a year's grain and seed.
I won't lead a life beyond measure.
Why should I have more than I need?
I pound sorghum to make home brew;
And drink until in wine I'm drowned.
Beside me plays my son of two,
Making inarticulate sound.
Such trifling things afford delight;
I forget the vainglorious age.
Gazing from afar on clouds white,
I seem to see the ancient sage.

和郭主簿

（二首其二）

和泽^①周^②三春^③，清凉素秋节。
露凝无游氛^④，天高肃景澈。
陵岑耸逸峰，遥瞻皆奇绝。
芳菊开林耀，青松冠岩列。
怀此贞秀姿，卓^⑤为霜下杰。
衔觞念幽人，千载抚^⑥尔诀^⑦。
检素不获展，厌厌竟良月。

① 和泽：风调雨顺，雨水丰沛。

② 周：遍及。

③ 三春：春天的三个月。即孟春，仲春，季春。

④ 游氛：飘动的云彩。

⑤ 卓：超出，不平凡，独立于群。

⑥ 抚：保持。

⑦ 诀：原则，规则，引申为节操，气节。

　　该首写秋色。诗人用逸峰、松菊暗指高人隐士。"秋凉素秋节"指秋季凉风萧瑟，象征着诗人清廉纯洁的品质；"陵岑耸逸峰"指秀逸山峰高大耸立，象征着诗人傲岸不屈的精神；"芳菊开林耀"指芳菊盛开处熠熠生辉，象征着诗人卓异于流俗的节操。诗人情不自禁怀想松菊坚贞秀美的英姿，赞叹其卓尔不群的风貌，赞誉其为霜下之杰。寓意诗人审美的主体意识，物我融一的精神境界。"检素不获展，厌厌竟良月。"指诗人的志向未得到施展，在清秋明月之下也不由得恹恹无绪，暗指诗人内心始终潜藏着一股壮志未酬而悲愤不平的内心世界。

In Reply to Secretary Guo

(II. Autumn)

Three spring moons abound in mild rain;

Now come the cool, pure autumn days.

No mist floats over dewy plain;

The sky sublime sheds limpid rays.

Peaks tower, mountains undulate,

What a wonderful far-off sight!

Chrysanthemums are golden mate

Of green pines crowning rocky height.

On their spirit I meditate:

Frost-proof, they are so brave and bright.

Cup in hand, I miss the recluse

Who loved blooms and pines long ago.

What have I done?

What could I choose?

I can only bend my head low.

癸卯岁十二月中作与从弟敬远

寝迹①衡门②下,邈与世相绝。

顾盼莫谁知,荆扉昼常闭。

凄凄岁暮风,翳翳③经日雪。

倾耳无希声,在目皓已洁④。

劲气侵襟袖,箪瓢⑤谢屡设。

萧索空宇中,了无一可悦。

历览千载书,时时见遗烈。

高操非所攀,谬⑥得固穷节。

平津⑦苟不由⑧,栖迟讵为拙!

寄意一言外,兹契⑨谁能别?

① 寝迹:埋没行踪,指隐居。
② 衡门:横木为门,指住处简陋。
③ 翳翳:昏暗的样子。
④ 皓已洁:即"已皓洁",此处是将副词"已"置于两个形容词之间的用法。
⑤ 箪(dān)瓢:即箪食瓢饮。箪:用于盛饭的竹器。瓢:葫芦剖开一半制成的舀水器具。
⑥ 谬:错误,谦辞。
⑦ 平津:平坦的大路,引申为仕途。津:渡口,此处指道路。
⑧ 由:沿着,遵循。
⑨ 契:契合,符合,这里指志同道合。

公元403年,陶渊明39岁。这首诗即丁忧家居时之作。敬远是渊明的同祖弟,这首诗借赠敬远以自抒情怀。作诗当月,桓玄篡晋称楚,把晋安帝迁禁在陶渊明的故乡寻阳。在统治阶级互相争夺严重的险恶环境中,诗人只能强作忘情,自求解脱之道,诗就是在这种背景下写的。

"邈与世相绝"说的是诗人因隐居而远离尘世与之相隔绝,其实并非真正隔绝,暗指是被黑暗局势逼迫的。"了无一可悦"说的是房中户外竟没有一件事是可以开心的,以婉转诙谐之笔写出穷困之境。"栖迟讵为拙"说的是隐居躬耕岂算拙?从另一层面表现了诗人的坚贞与超脱。"寄意一言外"说的是我寄深意在言外,诗人把悲愤沉痛和坚强,变成闲淡乐观和诙谐,陶诗的意境,自然达到了登峰造极的深厚和醇美。

For My Cousin Jingyuan

I've hidden in thatched cot secluded trace
From social life I stay far, far away.
Left and right I find no familiar face;
My wicket gate is closed e'en at midday.
The dreary wind mourns the end of the year;
From dawn till dusk falls a skyful of snow.
I listen but no sound reaches my ear;
I gaze but see dazzling light high and low.
Chilly air invades my collar and sleeves;
My table's often bare of drink and food.
In empty rooms only solitude grieves.
What's there to please?
Can there be nothing good?
I can peruse but books of olden days,
In which I find deeds worthy of memory.
I cannot climb the old time-honored ways,
Though wrongly praised for honest poverty.
If I can't follow the broad common road,
Is it bad a rural life to renew?
I tell you I will not leave my abode,
Who can understand me better than you?

始作镇军参军经曲阿作

弱龄寄事外，委怀在琴书。
被①褐欣自得，屡空常晏如②。
时③来苟④冥会⑤，宛辔⑥憩通衢。
投策⑦命晨装，暂与园田疏。
眇眇孤舟逝，绵绵归思纡⑧。
我行岂不遥，登降⑨千里余。
目倦川途异，心念山泽居。
望云惭高鸟，临水愧游鱼。
真想⑩初在襟，谁谓形迹拘？
聊且凭化迁，终返班生⑪庐。

① 被：同"披"，穿着。
② 晏如：安然快乐的样子。
③ 时：时机。
④ 苟：苟且，暂且。
⑤ 冥会：很自然的吻合。
⑥ 辔(pèi)：驾驭牲口的缰绳和嚼子。
⑦ 策：手杖。
⑧ 纡：魂牵梦绕。
⑨ 降：指穿过河流。
⑩ 真想：纯洁朴素的思想。
⑪ 班生：班固，东汉史学家、文学家。

公元 404 年，陶渊明 40 岁，为生活所迫，出任镇军将军刘裕的参军，赴京口（今江苏镇江）上任。往昔的生活经历使他对官场的黑暗已经有了十分深切的了解，口腹自役，这与作者的本性又格格不入，行经曲阿（今江苏丹阳）时，写下了这首诗，诉说内心的矛盾和苦闷。

全诗可分为 4 段。"弱龄寄事外，委怀在琴书"说的是年少时对世俗没有兴趣，只倾心于弹琴和读书，借指诗人年轻时就有淡泊自持之志。"宛辔憩通衢"说的是暂时栖身登仕途，说明诗人是迫不得已出仕的，认为与田园的分别是暂时的。"眇眇孤舟逝"说的是孤舟遥遥逐渐越来越远。表达了诗人不舍，又因充满了险恶风波的仕途而思归之情达到了极点，甚至看见飞鸟、游鱼内心不免产生后悔情绪，以及对此行的厌倦和自责情绪。"谁谓形迹拘"说的是岂会被拘束，诗人自我安慰鼓励自己，从后悔情绪中挣脱出来而对自我的重新肯定。随运顺化，终返田园。表现了诗人不喜不惧的道家人生态度，尽显真实思想和决心。

On My River Journey

While young, I used to be carefree,
Only indulged in lute and books.
Plain dress did not reduced my glee,
Nor did course food impair my looks.
As chance would have it, disinclined,
I drove up my official way.
Staff in hand, I made up my mind
To leave my garden for a day.
Far, far away goes my lonely boat;
Long, long my home thoughts haunt my heart.
Is it not a long journey afloat?
A thousand miles keep us apart.
Changing river scenes tire the eye;
Of hillside cot my mind still dreams.
Seeing birds and clouds, I feel shy
And envy fish swimming in streams.
To nature I've ever been true.
Who says my mind is matter-bound?
But the current I must go through,
Then in seclusion I'll be found.

乙巳岁三月为建威
参军使都经钱溪

我不践斯境,岁月好已积。

晨夕看山川,事事悉①如昔。

微雨洗高林,清飙矫②云翮③。

眷彼品物④存,义风⑤都未隔。

伊⑥余何为者,勉励从兹役?

一形⑦似有制⑧,素襟不可易。

园田日⑨梦想,安得久离析?

终怀在归舟⑩,谅哉宜霜柏。

① 悉:都。
② 矫:抬起,举起。
③ 翮(hé):指代鸟的翅膀。
④ 品物:万物。
⑤ 义风:适宜的风。
⑥ 伊:语气助词,无意义。
⑦ 一形:一身,即诗人本身。
⑧ 制:为……所制,限制。
⑨ 日:天天,每天。
⑩ 归舟:逯(lù)本作(逯钦立对《陶渊明集》的注释)"壑(hè)舟"。壑舟:深谷激流中的小舟,喻流逝不停的时间。语出《庄子·大宗师》:"夫藏舟于壑,藏山于泽,谓之固矣。然而夜半有力者负之而走,昧者不知也。"后以"壑舟"比喻在不知不觉中事物不停地变化、迁移。

公元405年,陶渊明41岁。年初,陶渊明担任江州刺史刘敬宣(建威将军)的参军,三月奉差使去京都建康,这诗是途中泊舟于钱溪(今安徽省贵池东梅根港)所作。"事事悉如昔"指事事未变如往昔,说明诗人曾经来过这里,旧地重游。"素襟不可易"指平素的胸襟是不可改变的。诗人触景生情、寓情于景的手法来表达想要归隐田园的意念,暗指退出仕途的决心。"谅哉宜霜柏"指霜中松柏自挺立,表达诗人像霜后的松柏一样,保持着高尚的情操和品德。

Qian Stream Revisited

How long have I not visited here?
Days have piled up into a year.
Dawn to dusk I see hills and streams,
Scenes are revived as in old dreams.
In fine rain steeped the branches high,
Wind-borne birds ripple cloudy sky.
That's what a familiar eye sees,
Not saddened by a heartfelt breeze.
Why should I plod along the way,
Tied down to my post all the day?
My body seems bound up in view,
But I've a heart none could subdue.
I miss my rural life and song.
Could I be kept away for long?
In homing boat I'd be carefree,
Oh, as a frost-proof cypress tree.

归去来①兮②辞

① 来：助词，无义。
② 兮：语气词，无义。

归去来兮，田园将芜胡不归？
既自以心为形役，奚③惆怅而独悲！
悟以往之不谏④，知来者之可追⑤。
实迷途其未远，觉今是而昨非。
舟遥遥⑥以轻飏⑦，风飘飘而吹衣。
问征夫以前路，恨⑧晨光之熹微。
乃瞻衡宇，载欣载⑨奔。
僮仆欢迎，稚子候门。

③ 奚：为什么。
④ 谏：劝谏，挽回。
⑤ 追：追回，补救。
⑥ 遥遥：顺着水流飘荡的样子。
⑦ 飏(yáng)：形容船在水中行驶的轻快。
⑧ 恨：遗憾。
⑨ 载……载……：一边……一边……

　　公元 405 年，陶渊明 41 岁。诗人从 29 岁起开始出仕，任官 13 年，一直厌恶官场，向往田园。在 41 岁时，最后一次出仕，做了 80 多天的彭泽令即辞官回家，以后再也没有出来做官。辞官后并作得此诗，以明心志。（辞前有序，说明了诗人出仕和自免去职的原因。本文直见正文，在此略序。）

　　"归去来兮"开门见山，意为"回家去吧！"，第一段表现出诗人对人生的大彻大悟及归田之决心。在诗人的意识中，田园是人类生命的根，是自由生活的象征。他看穿了官场的污浊，不愿同流合污；认识到仕途即迷途，幸而践之未远，回头不迟；一种悔悟和庆幸之情溢于言表。

　　"乃瞻衡宇，载欣载奔"说的是诗人一看见家门，高兴得奔跑，尽显天真。第二段可以看出诗人归家后僮仆、孩子、妻子欣喜并做隆重欢

Home-Going-and-Coming Song

Let me go home!
Oh, why should I still roam
While my fields will be overgrown with weed,
Why don't I go where there is need?
Since I allowed my body to be master of my mind,
Why should my service be considered as unkind?
Let the bygone days be bygone!
The future's still my own.
I've not gone far astray,
Now that I know I was wrong yesterday.
My boat and ripples sway;
My robe flaps with breeze light.
I ask my homeward way,
And wait to see twilight.
Seeing my cot with glee,
I'm afraid to be late.
My household welcomes me
With children at the gate.

三径就①荒，松菊犹存。

携幼入室，有酒盈樽。

引壶觞以自酌，眄②庭柯以怡颜。

倚南窗以寄傲，审容膝③之易安。

园日涉以成趣，门虽设而常关。

策④扶老⑤以流憩⑥，时矫首而遐观。

云无心以出岫，鸟倦飞而知还。

景翳翳以将入，抚孤松而盘桓⑦。

归去来兮，请息交以绝游。

世与我而相违，复驾言兮焉求？

① 就：接近，就要。

② 眄(miǎn)：斜着看，这里指随便看看。

③ 容膝：只容得下膝盖的地方，形容房子很小。

④ 策：拄着。

⑤ 扶老：手杖。

⑥ 流憩：到处走走歇歇。

⑦ 盘桓：徘徊，舍不得离开。

迎以及诗人的愉悦之情。看见园中景色，使诗人欣慰于自己本性的犹存，写尽饮酒自乐和傲然自得的情景。有贤淑的妻子、温馨的家庭，表明知足常乐之态亦有孤介傲岸之势。

"归去来兮，请息交以绝游"说的是"回来呀，我要跟世俗之人断绝交游"。第三段借景抒情，诗人羡慕自然界的万物一到春天便生长茂盛，感叹自己的一生行将结束。

The paths look like wasteland
But for chrysanthemum and pine.
I enter, holding my youngest son's hand,
And see my cup brimming with wine.
I freely drink unoccupied
And gaze with smile at courtyard trees.
Standing by the window with pride,
In narrow rooms I feel at ease.
I walk in my garden with pleasure;
The gate is closed without a bar.
Wandering, staff in hand, at leisure,
I look upward and afar.
Carefree clouds leave the mountain crest,
Tired birds fly back towards their nest.
The sun is dimmed on its decline
And I caress a lonely pine.
I'm now at home,
In mundane world I'll no more roam.
Since social life and I cannot agree,
What can I seek to do if I want to be free?

悦亲戚之情话，乐琴书以消忧。

农人告余以春及，将有事于西畴。

或命巾车，或棹孤舟。

既窈窕①以寻壑，亦崎岖而经丘。

木欣欣以向荣，泉涓涓而始流。

善万物之得时，感吾生之行休②。

已矣乎③，

寓形④宇内⑤复几时？

曷⑥不委心⑦任去留⑧？

胡为乎遑遑⑨欲何之？

富贵非吾愿，帝乡不可期。

① 窈(yáo)窕(tiǎo)：形容山谷幽深曲折的样子。

② 行休：生命将要结束。

③ 已矣乎：算了吧！此处语气助词连用，加强感叹。

④ 寓形：寄托生命。

⑤ 宇内，天地之间。

⑥ 曷(hé)：何，为什么。

⑦ 委心：随心之自然，顺遂自心。

⑧ 去留：指人的生死。

⑨ 遑遑：心里忐忑不安的样子。

"已矣乎！寓形宇内复几时"说的是"算了吧！活在世上还能有多久？"。诗人否定了世俗政治社会，亦摒弃了宗教彼岸世界，要在自己的生活中求得人生之意义、实现人生之价值，让自己的生命始终顺应自然之道，是诗人的理想人生。诗人的人生态度是认真的、现世的，这是超越的境界，同时也是脚踏实地的。

Talking with kins will bring me pleasure;
Reading and playing lute beguile my leisure.
I'm told by farmers of the coming of season best
For me to till the field in the west.
I drive a cart
Or row a boat.
To go across rugged hills I start,
Or on a winding stream I float.
With joy all flowers blow;
Slowly streams glide from fountains clear.
In time all the things move and grow;
To the end my life's drawing near.
So let it be!
How long on earth can I do what I please?
Why not set my mind free?
Where should I go?
Why ill at ease?
I do not aspire to wealth or renown,
Nor go up to celestial spheres.

怀良辰以孤往，或植杖而耘耔。
登东皋以舒啸，临清流而赋诗。
聊乘化以归尽，乐夫天命复奚疑！

I only wish to wander on my own
Or leave my staff to till the field where weed appears.
I'll go up eastern hill to sing
Or croon a verse by limpid stream.
I'll return to the source of spring
And vanish with sunshine or moonbeam.

形 影 神

（三首其一：形赠影）

天地长不没，山川无改时。

草木得常理，霜露荣悴之①。

谓人最灵智，独复不如兹。

适②见在世中，奄去③靡归期。

奚④觉无一人，亲识岂相思？

但余平生物，举目情凄洏⑤。

我无腾化术，必尔不复疑。

愿君取吾言，得酒莫苟⑥辞！

① 荣悴之：使它盛开与凋零。之：指草木。

② 适：刚刚，刚才。

③ 奄去：突然消失，指死亡。

④ 奚：谁。

⑤ 洏(ér)：眼泪流下的样子。

⑥ 苟：轻率，随意。

　　这三首诗大约作于公元413年，陶渊明当时49岁。形神问题是中国哲学中的一个重要命题，陶渊明笃守先世崇奉之天师道信仰，故以道家自然观为立论之本。既不同于魏晋时期的自然崇仰者，又不同于魏晋时期的尊奉孔孟、标举名教者；而诗人既接受了老庄的思想，又有感于晋宋之际的社会现实，于是创作一种新的自然说。故用寓言的形式以形、影、神三者之间的相互问答来展开论述，可谓奇思异想，令这一哲学上的讨论富有生动活泼的意趣，而在这三首诗中亦表达了他的人生哲学。

　　"天地长不没，山川无改时"，形体对影子说天地长久，永远不会湮灭，山川走形，永远不会变更。"谓人最灵智，独复不如兹"说的是身为万物之灵的人类却不能如此。然而人活在世上，就像匆匆的过客，之前还在世间相见，可转眼就去了另一个世界，于这个大世界来说，走了一个人，

Body, Shadow and Spirit

(Body to Shadow)

The sky and earth will last forever;
Streams flow and mountains spread as ever.
As a rule, drooping plants may renew,
Withered by frost and revived by dew.
If man is the wisest of all,
Can he not know who rise will fall?
A man whom we have seen before
May die at once and is no more.
But who will take note of his death for long?
Even his kins have no memory strong.
Only the things he left before their eyes
May draw from them sad tears and drear sighs.
To be immortal I don't know the art,
Nor do I doubt of my allotted part.
I wish you would remember what I say
And drink our cup of wine without delay.

不会引起他人的注意，但是亲戚朋友，哪有不思念的！形体说自己没有飞天成仙的本领，影子也不必怀疑我最终的归宿，劝告影子在醉乡寻求暂时的欢乐。诗人依托旧自然说的观点展现对话，其主旨在于说明人生之短暂，不如自然之永恒。

形 影 神

（三首其二：影答形）

存生不可言，卫生每苦拙。
诚愿游昆华①，邈然兹道绝。
与子相遇来，未尝异悲悦。
憩荫若暂乖②，止日③终不别。
此同既难常，黯尔④俱时灭。
身没名亦尽，念之五情⑤热。
立善⑥有遗爱，胡为不自竭？
酒云能消忧，方此讵⑦不劣？

① 昆华：昆仑山和华山，传说中神仙居住的地方。

② 乖：分开。

③ 止日：在太阳下。

④ 黯尔：黯然无光，心神十分沮丧的样子。

⑤ 五情：泛指人的感情。

⑥ 立善：时有三不朽：立言、立功、立德，三者总称立善。

⑦ 讵(jù)：难道。

这首诗为影子回答形体"存生不可言，卫生每苦拙"，指想寻求长生不老来维持生命是不可靠的，但是保养生命健康，也很苦恼，没有好的方法。影子以依托主名教者的口吻而对旧自然说提出其对人生的看法，长生不可期，神仙不可求，意在指责主自然说观点的那些人的虚无荒诞。"立善有遗爱"，因人死生无常，名同身亡，故主张由立善而留名，希望通过精神上的长生来达到永恒，美名得以流芳百世，万古长存。

Body, Shadow and Spirit

(Shadow to Body)

A man's life cannot last forever;
It is hard even to live long.
You like immortal land as ever.
Can you tell the way not to go wrong?
Our companionship may not fade,
For we have shared same joy and pain.
If I have left you in the shade,
In sunshine I'll appear again.
We can't get together forever;
In time we both shall disappear.
Could I stay when you are gone? Never.
Thinking of this, I'm sad and drear.
But good deeds will be left tomorrow.
Why then do you not do your best?
Though drinking may drive away sorrow,
What good has wine done to your rest?

形 影 神

（三首其三：神释）

大钧无私力，万理自森著。

人为三才①中，岂不以我故?

与君虽异物，生而相依附。

结托既喜同，安得不相语?

三皇②大圣人，今复在何处?

彭祖③爱永年④，欲留不得住。

老少同一死，贤愚无复数⑤。

日醉或能忘，将非⑥促龄⑦具⑧?

①三才：指天、地、人。

②三皇：古代传说中的三个帝王，说法不一，通常认为是神农、伏羲、燧人。

③彭祖：古代传说中的长寿者，生于夏代，一直活到了周朝，总共八百岁。爱：当是"受"字之讹(é)，意思是彭祖享受了八百岁高龄。

④永年：长寿。

⑤数：气数，命运。

⑥将非：岂非，难道不是。

⑦促龄：促使人的寿命变短。

⑧具：器具，指酒。

"大钧无私力，万理自森著"指大自然的造化没有偏爱谁，万物都按照自己的规律成长繁衍。而人类能跻身于天地人三才之中，也是因为神的缘故，神说自己与形和影虽然不相同，但生来就互相依附。就像与朋友对话一样说出自己的看法，"三皇大圣人，今复在何处"古时的三皇被称作大圣人，而今他们却在何处？其意在诋斥代表主名教者——影鼓吹的立善留名可以不朽的说法；"彭祖爱永年"意在破除代表主旧自然说者——形的长生求仙与沉湎醉乡的言论；最后提出纵浪大化，随顺自然；"应尽便须尽，无复独多虑"听从老天的安排吧，不必多虑。

这首诗即体现了诗人新自然说的主张，又借神的话批评了代表旧自然说的形和代表名教说的影，可谓妙哉！

Body, Shadow and Spirit

(Spirit)

Impartial is Heaven's power high,
All things follow its laws divine.
Man levels up with earth and sky.
Is it not due to power mine?
Different beings as we are.
Still we're Three united in One.
We live and die under same star,
And know how to end what's begun.
The three great emperors were sages,
But where can they be found today?
The oldest Peng had lived eight ages,
Bald could not have a longer stay.
Young and old will die in the end;
Wit and fool may have the same fate.
Wine may make you forget, not mend.
Won't it make death precipitate?

立善常所欣，谁当为汝誉？
甚念伤吾生，正宜委运①去。
纵浪②大化③中，不喜亦不惧。
应尽便须尽，无④复独多虑！

① 委运：顺遂自然。
② 纵浪：放任自由，不受拘束。
③ 大化：宇宙，大自然。
④ 无：同"毋"，不要。

Doing good will gladden your mind.
Who'll sing after your death your praise?
Do not think of things of such kind,
But follow nature in future days.
Play with rising or ebbing tide
Without pleasure and without fear!
Enjoy sunny as shady side!
Let things appear and disappear!

九日闲居

世短意常多，斯人①乐久生。　　①斯人：人人。
日月依辰至，举②俗爱其名。　　②举：整个，全部。
露凄暄风③急，气澈天象明。　　③暄风：温暖的风。
往燕无遗影，来雁有余声。
酒能祛百虑，菊解制颓龄④。　　④颓龄：暮年。
如何蓬庐士，空视时运倾⑤。　　⑤倾：斜，引申为变迁。
尘爵耻虚罍，寒华徒自荣。　　⑥栖迟：隐居而游玩休憩的意思。
敛襟独闲谣，缅焉起深情。　　　栖：住宿；迟：迟缓。
栖迟⑥固多娱，淹留岂无成⑦！　⑦淹留岂无成：反用《楚辞·九辨》"蹇(jiǎn)淹留而无成"，意思是长期归隐，难道就会一事无成？淹留：长时间停留，指长期隐退。

公元419年或之后，此时陶渊明已过55岁。据《宋书·陶潜传》记载陶渊明归隐后闲居家中，某年九月九日重阳节，宅边的菊花正开，然因家贫无酒，正在惆怅感伤之际，忽然时任江州刺史的王宏派人送来了酒，诗人也不推辞，开怀畅饮。"世短意常多"指人生促促，其意在表达人生在世不过白驹过隙，诗中"九"通"久"，人们对它的喜爱体现了对长生的渴求，诗人以九月九来感叹人生。"尘爵耻虚罍，寒华徒自荣"指诗人感叹自己有菊无酒，空负良辰美景，暗指诗人贫寒潦倒的处境和已经寥落的心情。"敛襟独闲谣"指整理衣襟独自悠然歌咏，说明诗人对人生价值有了新的审视，暗喻了他对晋宋易代的悲愤，以及对前朝的留恋。

Written at Leisure on Double Ninth Day

Life is short, full of cares and sighs;
On earth men still wish to live long.
In time sun and moon sink and rise
But we like the Double Ninth song.
The wind won't sough on dreary dew;
The fresh air makes the sky more clear.
Parting swallows leave no shadow new;
Honking wild geese don't reach the ear.
Drinking may drive all cares away;
Chrysanthemums prolong our life.
Living in thatched cot night and day;
I still neglect the world in strife.
Cups would feel ashamed without wine;
Unenjoyed flowers bloom in vain.
Donning my robe, I croon verse line;
Deep thoughts may lead to joy or pain.
Enjoying solitude with pleasure,
I'm happy in my life of leisure.

归园田居

（五首其一）

少①无适俗韵，性本爱丘山。　　①少：年轻的时候。
误落尘网中，一去②三十年，　　②去：离开。
羁鸟恋旧林，池鱼思故渊。
开荒南野际，守拙③归园田。　　③守拙：坚守节操。
方宅十余亩，草屋八九间。
榆柳荫后檐，桃李罗堂前。
暧暧④远人村，依依⑤墟里⑥烟。　　④暧暧：朦胧的样子。
　　　　　　　　　　　　　　　⑤依依：轻柔缓慢地升起。
狗吠深巷中，鸡鸣桑树颠。　　　⑥墟里：村庄。
户庭无尘杂，虚室有余闲。
久在樊笼⑦里，复得返自然。　　⑦樊笼：鸟笼，这里比喻官场生活。

　　公元405年，陶渊明在江西彭泽辞官后，回到家中作《归园田居》诗一组，共五首，描绘田园风光的美好与农村生活的淳朴愉悦，以及归隐后的心情。对于诗人来说，人生的道路只有两条任他选择：一条是出仕做官，有俸禄保证其生活，可是必须违心地与世俗同流合污；另一条是归隐田园，靠躬耕劳动维持生存，这样可以做到任性存真、坚持操守。

　　"误落尘网中"指错误地落入仕途罗网，反映诗人对官场生活的厌倦。"守拙归园田"指依着拙朴的心性归耕田园。诗人以近景和远景来投射出乡村的幽静逍遥与上层社会的虚伪欺诈形成鲜明对比。"复得返自然"总算又归返林山；诗人三次着重强调归田之心，体现诗人精神上的追求是自由和独立的。

Return to Nature

(I)

While young, I was not used to worldly cares,
And hills became my natural compeers.
But by mistake I fell in mundane snares,
And was thus entangled for thirteen years.
A caged bird would long for wonted wood,
And fish in ponds for native pools would yearn.
Go back to till my southern field I would,
To live a rural life why not return?
My plot of ground is but ten acres square;
My thatched cottage has eight or nine rooms.
In front I have peach trees here and plums there;
Over back eaves willows and elms cast glooms.
A village can be seen in distant dark,
Where plumes of smoke rise and waft in the breeze.
In alley deep a dog is heard to bark,
And cocks crow as if over mulbery trees.
Into my courtyard no one should intrude,
Nor rob my private rooms of peace and leisure.
After long, long official servitude,
Again in nature I find homely pleasure.

归园田居

（五首其二）

野外罕人事，穷巷寡轮鞅①。
白日掩荆扉，虚室绝尘想。
时复墟曲②中，披③草共来往。
相见无杂言，但道桑麻长。
桑麻日已长，我土日已广。
常恐霜霰至，零落同草莽。

① 轮鞅：指车马。
② 墟曲：田野。
③ 披：拨开。

"虚室绝尘想"指独处在空室中不生杂想，暗含摆脱世俗束缚的喜悦。"相见无杂言，但道桑麻长"指相见时不谈论世俗之事，只说道桑麻的生长情况。诗人是喜悦的，诗人的乡居生活总体来说是平静安宁的，但是他的心情也会有喜有忧。"常恐霜霰至，零落同草莽"，诗人生怕自己辛勤劳动的成果毁于一旦，心怀恐惧，说明了作者此时心中亦乐亦忧的乃是作物与耕地，展现了诗人明澈的心灵，纯朴的感情。

Return to Nature

(II)

In countryside few care about the State,
Nor Wheels nor hooves are heard in the deep gloom.
By broad daylight I close my wicket gate;
No worldly dust invades my vacant room.
Sometimes I go along the winding way
And meet with peasants through the bushy field.
Then we have nothing untoward to say
But talk about our corn's growth and its yield.
Our corn grows day by day under our feet;
My field becomes wider beyond wild grass.
But I fear the onset of frost and sleet
Would do harm to my corn and grain, alas!

归园田居

（五首其三）

种豆南山下，草盛豆苗稀。
晨兴理荒秽，带月荷①锄归。　　① 荷：扛着。
道狭草木长，夕露沾我衣。
衣沾不足惜，但使愿无违。

　　"种豆南山下，草盛豆苗稀"说的是南山下田野里种植豆子，结果是草茂盛豆苗稀疏，说明诗人对耕种缺乏经验。但诗人却未灰心丧气，甚至在田地里从早忙到晚。"带月荷锄归"说的是暮色降、披月光扛锄回去，体现了中华民族自古以来的吃苦耐劳，坚韧不拔的精神。"夕露沾我衣"显示出了从事农业劳动的艰苦，同时表明诗人终生归隐的意愿，虽辛苦但很愉快。"衣沾不足惜，但使愿无违。"说明陶渊明不在乎衣服被露水打湿，尽管田园生活很艰苦，可是诗人却愿意在这样的田园生活中回归自我，而不让自己迷失在黑暗的官场，保持着心灵的纯洁，体现诗人超脱于世俗的精神境界。

Return to Nature

(III)

I sow my beans 'neath Southern Hill,

Bean shoots are lost where weeds o'er grow.

I weed at dawn though early still;

I plod home with my moonlit hoe.

The path is narrow, grasses tall,

With evening dew my clothes wet.

To which I pay no heed at all,

If my desire can but be met.

归园田居

（五首其四）

久去山泽游，浪莽①林野娱。　　①浪莽：空旷。
试携子侄辈，披榛步荒墟。
徘徊丘垄间，依依②昔人居。　　②依依：隐约。
井灶有遗处，桑竹残杇③株。　　③杇（wū）：粉刷。
借问采薪者，此人皆焉如④？　　④焉如：到哪里去了。
薪者向我言，死没⑤无复余。　　⑤没：死。一作"殁"。
一世⑥异朝市，此语真不虚。　　⑥一世：三十年为一世。
人生似幻化，终当归空无。

"久去山泽游"指离山泽去做官已经很久，说明诗人归田已经有一段时日了，同时也是对误落尘网中的回顾。"试携子侄辈，披榛步荒墟"，携着我的儿女侄子们拨开树丛漫步荒墟；诗人与家人同游，可见其游兴之浓，而句末的"荒墟"二字承上启下，引出了后面的所见、所问、所感。通过描写游历废墟以及同砍柴人之间的对答，表达了诗人不胜沧桑、人生无常的感慨。"人生似幻化，终当归空无"阐释着人生有盛则有衰、有生则有死这样一个无可逃避的事物规律和自然法则。诗句看似平平淡淡，但所蕴藏的哲理意义极深，从中可以看到诗人内心的境界、智慧的灵光及其对世事、人生的了悟。

Return to Nature

(IV)

Having long left hills and streams, how
I love to roam in woody place!
Coming with sons and nephews, now
Through hazels I see ruined trace.
I pace up and down on waste land
And find debris of dwellers old.
Marks of old wells and stoves still stand,
Dead branches are left in the cold.
I ask a woodman passing by,
If he knows who lived here before.
The woodman answers with a sigh,
"They are all dead and gone, no more."
Thirty years passed in town and court.
Everything has changed, it is true.
Life is a vison fair and short;
All will vanish into the blue.

归园田居
(五首其五)

怅恨独策还,崎岖历榛曲。
山涧清且浅,可以濯吾足。
漉①我新熟酒,只鸡招近局②。
日入室中暗,荆薪代明烛。
欢来苦夕短,已复至天旭。

① 漉:过滤。
② 近局:邻居。

    这首诗以一天耕作完毕之后,回家的路上和到家之后的活动作为描写对象,来反映"归园田居"后的另一个生活侧面。"怅恨独策还,崎岖历榛曲"指诗人怀着怅恨情拄杖回家,崎岖的小路上长满荆榛,暗指当时社会动荡不安所致道路的荒凉和艰难。"濯吾足"指清洗沾染尘埃的双脚,表明归隐之志坚持不改之意。之后诗人备好自酿新熟酒,自饲之家鸡,邀上邻友共酌共饮,即觉足矣,这正是诗人欢喜的淳朴的农家生活。"欢来苦夕短,已复至天旭",诗人兴致难尽,直至旭日渐升天方肯作罢,诗人以寄其高远之志,抒其胸中超然之情。

Return to Nature

(V)

Melancholy, I come back, staff in hand,

Going alone the rugged bushy way.

In mountain crooks shallow and clear I stand

And wash my feet where a moment I stay.

At home I strain my newly-ripened wine,

Cook a chicken and with neighbors share it.

My room turns dark when there's no more sunshine,

Branches are burned instead of candle lit.

So joyful we're that we find short the night;

Soon in the east we see the first sunlight.

乞 食

饥来驱我去,不知竟何之^①!
行行至斯里,叩门拙言辞^②。
主人解余意,遗赠岂虚来^③。
谈话终日夕,觞至辄^④倾杯。
情欣新知欢,言咏遂赋诗。
感子^⑤漂母惠^⑥,愧我非韩才。
衔戢^⑦知何谢,冥报^⑧以相贻。

① 何之:去哪里。
② 拙言辞:拙于言辞,不知该说些什么。
③ 岂虚来:怎么能让你白跑一趟。
④ 辄(zhé):就。
⑤ 子:对人的尊称。
⑥ 漂母惠:像漂母那样的恩惠。漂母,河边洗衣的妇女。《史记·淮阴侯列传》:韩信穷苦的时候在河边钓鱼,洗衣服的妇人见他可怜,每次给他带来一些吃的,韩信立誓将来一定要报答这位老妇。在韩信灭项羽功成名就之后,韩信故地重游,赐老妇以千金。
⑦ 衔戢(jí):深藏于心,表示由衷的感谢。衔:马勒衔于口不会掉落,比喻永不忘。戢:收藏。
⑧ 冥报:死后在阴间报答。

关于这首诗的创作时间有两种说法,一是公元385年诗人21岁,与朋友聚会饮酒赋诗;二是公元426年诗人62岁,根据乞食的真实经历,写下此诗。这首诗不仅比较真实地反映了陶渊明晚年贫困生活的一个侧面,也真实地反映出陶渊明朴拙直率的个性。"乞食"在齐人不食嗟来之食的美谈中,是令人脸红耳热的字眼,诗人写了出来,并将诗中的启示意义超越了乞食一事。"饥来驱我去,不知竟何之"说明诗人是因本能的需求迫使其出门求食,并将诗人乞食时的心态、窘相刻画得惟妙惟肖。"新交好友心欢畅"表达诗人因结识到心地善良的主人而转忧为喜,其意是颂扬那些用真情和友善温暖他人的老百姓们。"死后报答君恩惠"表达诗人高尚的人格,知恩图报,饮水不忘挖井人,这是中华民族精神中的传统美德。

Begging for Food

Driven by hunger, I go out
But I do not know whereabout.
I plod on and on till this land;
I knock and speechless there I stand.
The host, seeing my hidden pain,
Gives me food lest I'd come in vain.
We talk until the sun's decline;
We empty cup on cup of wine.
I'm glad to make acquaintance new;
I write this verse as it is due.
I can't repay like Han Xin* fed
By a washerwoman her bread.
How to express my hearty thanks?
In underworld on griefless banks**.

---

* While young, Han Xin (2nd century B.C.) was fed by a washerwoman. When he became a general, he repaid her kindness with gold.
** It was believed in ancient China that there was a Griefless River in the underworld.

连雨独饮

运生会归尽,终古谓之然。
世间有松乔①,于今定何间?
故老赠余酒,乃②言饮得仙。
试酌百情远,重觞忽忘天。
天岂去此哉?任真③无所先。
云鹤有奇翼,八表④须臾⑤还。
自我抱兹独⑥,僶俛四十年。
形骸久已化,心在复何言!

① 松乔:神话传说中仙人赤松子与王子乔。
② 乃:竟然。
③ 任真:顺其自然。
④ 八表:八方之外的地方,形容很远的地方。
⑤ 须臾:片刻。
⑥ 独:指"任真"。

公元 404 年,陶渊明 40 岁。此诗在饮酒中议论人生哲理。诗人坚信自然界的规律是有生必有死,世间并无长生久视的神仙,人应该听任自然,顺应自然的发展规律。诗中既表达人生态度,也表达愿独守"任真"的信念。这是一首饮酒诗,亦是一首哲理诗。"运生会归尽,终古谓之然"指人在自然运化中有生必会有死,自古以来都是如此,说明诗人进一步思索应该采取的人生态度。"试酌百情远"一句中,诗人借助饮酒的刺激体验到的断离杂念的境界,如果人能忘情忘我,也就达到了与物为一、与自然运化为一体的境界。"形骸久已化,心在复何言"指身体虽然不断变化,"任真"之心还有什么忧虑可言呢?一语收回,即表人生态度,又引人深思。

Drinking Alone on Rainy Nights

Where there's life, there will be death:
This truth is well known since old days.
Where can we find immortal breath
Exhaled in superhuman ways?
Old friends tell me a jar of wine
Would make me forget weal and woe.
After drinking nectar divine,
Even to Heaven I won't go.
Is Heaven far from our good earth?
Following nature, you'll go high.
The crane in cloud with wings of worth
Flies to and fro from earth to sky.
I have been firm in my belief
And in my life for forty years.
My mind is free of joy and grief,
Though long my body changed appears.

移 居

（二首其一）

昔欲居南村，非为卜其宅。

闻多素心人，乐与数晨夕。

怀此颇有年，今日从兹役。

弊庐何必广，取足蔽床席。

邻曲时时来，抗言①谈在昔。

奇文共欣赏，疑义相与析。

① 抗言：直言。抗：同"亢"，高的意思。

因两年前的六月，诗人在上京之居遭遇火灾，房屋焚毁。公元410年九月后，又迁居南村，实现了他向往已久的愿望。当时诗人46岁，这首诗是这次迁居后的抒怀之作。"昔欲居南村"指诗人很早之前就想到南村居住了，后面写出了因那里的人纯朴，为此想要迁居的原因。"奇文共欣赏，疑义相与析"指美妙的文章可以共同欣赏，疑难问题可以互相分析，表达了诗人迁居后的乐趣，写出个人美好的理想同时，也曲折地暴露了当时社会政治的黑暗，体现诗人洁身自好，不与腐朽的统治者同流合污。

Moving House

(I)

In Southern Village I would dwell,
Not that the house there augurs well,
But people live in simple ways,
With whom I'm glad to pass my days.
For years I've cherished this ideal;
Today it becomes true and real.
Why should I need a spacious flat
But room enough for bed and mat?
My neighbors may call now or then,
And talk of olden days and men.
We'll read good writings we enjoy
And solve the questions which annoy.

戊申岁六月中遇火

草庐寄穷巷,甘以辞华轩。

正夏长风急,林室顿烧燔①。

一宅无遗宇,舫舟荫门前。

迢迢新秋夕,亭亭②月将圆。

果菜始复生,惊鸟尚未还。

中宵伫遥念,一盼周九天。

总发③抱孤介④,奄⑤出⑥四十年。

形迹⑦凭化往⑧,灵府⑨长独闲。

贞刚自有质,玉石乃⑩非坚。

① 燔(fán):焚烧。
② 亭亭:高远的样子。
③ 总发:总角,即童年。
④ 孤介:保持节操,不肯同流合污。
⑤ 奄:突然,忽然。
⑥ 出:超过。
⑦ 形迹:身体,引申为生命。
⑧ 往:变化。
⑨ 灵府:心灵。
⑩ 乃:却。

公元 408 年,陶渊明 44 岁,居住在上京,六月中旬一场大火烧毁了他家的房子,使他陷入了窘困的境地,只好住在门前的船中。房屋焚毁好似并没有使诗人感到更多的痛苦,他安居在船上,依然悠然地生活,秋天的时候写下了这首诗。

"草庐寄穷巷,甘以辞华轩"指茅屋盖在僻巷边,甘愿辞掉仕宦生活,说明诗人自愿的态度及平静的心情。"中宵伫遥念,一盼周九天"指半夜里诗人伫立遥想,一眼就遍观四周天。接着便开始了回顾自述平生操行,说明遇火后诗人心情不平静,房屋烧毁给了诗人沉重的打击。"既已不遇兹,且遂灌我园"指既然已经遇不上这样的时代了,还是灌耕我的田园吧;回到眼前的现实心情又平静下来了,这表现了诗人面对现实的态度。

My Cottage Caught Fire in Midsummer

Living in thatched cot down shabby lane,
I loved it more than house of golden frames.
A mid-summer blast blew with might and main,
My hut in the glade was swept by the flames.
My rooms were all burned up and lost to sight,
So in a boat I sought for shelter soon.
Long, long lasts the new autumn night,
Bright, bright shines the nearly full moon.
Again vegetables begin to grow,
But frightened birds won't come back here.
Far, far away my thoughts at midnight go,
When I gaze on the ninth celestial sphere.
While young, I loved to hold my own,
In that way I've passed forty years.
My body follows up and down,
My mind to independence steers.
It's pure and strong in its own way,
Like jade or stone which is fire-proof.

仰想东户时，余粮宿中田。
鼓腹无所思，朝起暮归眠。
既已不遇兹，且遂灌我园。

Looking up, I think of old day
With crops not stored under the roof.
People well-fed were carefree then.
They rose at dawn and slept at night.
Such golden age won't come again,
I would till my land if I might.

饮 酒
（二十首其一）

哀荣无定在，彼此更共之。
邵生①瓜田中，宁似东陵时？
寒暑有代谢，人道每如兹。
达人②解其会③，逝④将不复疑。
忽⑤与一觞酒，日夕欢相持。

① 邵生：邵平，秦朝的时候是东陵侯，秦朝灭亡了成了平民，因家贫而在长安城东种瓜。

② 达人：通达事理的人。

③ 会：道理的所在。

④ 逝：逝去，离开，这里指归隐田园。

⑤ 忽：快快地。

　　公元 416 年，刘裕调集全国的兵力，从东向西，分五路讨伐后秦。刘裕通过北伐，极大扩大了他个人的权力。朝廷为了讨好刘裕，可谓想要什么朝廷就给什么。陶渊明早就看透，东晋的气数已尽，刘裕篡位只是迟早的事，诗人整天为这件事悲伤郁闷，后又想一切都在发展变化中，为这些事烦恼也没有用，还是多喝点酒，好好睡一觉吧，于是就有了《饮酒》这组诗。这组诗非一时之作，从诗中有关景物环境的描写来看，这组诗大约是写于同一年的秋冬之际。诗人多方面地反映了自己的生活、思想、志趣与情操。

　　"哀荣无定在，彼此更共之"指衰落与荣盛不是固定的，双方是不断变更互相转化的，比喻人生的衰与盛、祸与福。"寒暑有代谢，人道每如兹"指寒来暑往有更替变化，人生也是如此。道出人生的道理和规律。

Wine-drinking Song

(I)

All men who rise will then decline,
Such is your fate as well as mine.
The melon-grower in the field
Was noble lord who would not yield.
Winter replaces summer days,
Such is the world and all men's ways.
The wise men who find the truth out,
Will not again put it in doubt.
Fill our cups of wine with delight,
Be intoxicated day and night!

饮 酒

(二十首其四)

栖栖失林鸟,日暮犹独飞。

徘徊无定止,夜夜声转悲。

厉响思清远,去来何所依?

因值①孤生松,敛翮遥来归。　　①值:遇到。

劲风无荣木,此荫独不衰。

托身已得所,千载不相违。

　　"栖栖失群鸟,日暮犹独飞"指黄昏时一只离群的鸟还在独自飞翔,形单影只,诗人用飞鸟比喻自己前半生的栖栖惶惶,暗喻自己从误落尘网到归隐田居的过程,及对现实的不满与对远离尘嚣的田园生活。"托身已得所,千载不相违"指既然得到了寄身之处,便永远相依不违弃。"因植孤生松",诗人以孤松比喻自己的归隐之所来表达自己矢志不渝的心念。

Wine-drinking Song

(IV)

A lonely, dreary bird astray
Still flies near the end of the day.
It hovers here and there, its cries
Have darkened night and saddened skies.
Is it longing for morning clear
Or a resting tree far or near?
Seeing a pine of towering height,
Folding its wings, it will alight.
No tree can stand a furious blast,
Which this shady pine can outlast.
The bird has found on it a nest,
For a long time here it will rest.

饮 酒
（二十首其五）

结庐在人境，而无车马喧。
问君何能尔，心远地自偏。
采菊东篱下，悠然见南山。
山气日夕佳，飞鸟相与还。
此中有真意，欲辨已忘言。

"结庐在人境，而无车马喧"指置身人境，能做到不染世俗之事，说明诗人的心和所处的环境都是静的，实际上是讲生活在现实中的人能否超脱于现实之外的问题。"采菊东篱下，悠然见南山"指诗人采菊东篱，悠然自得，此时的诗人超然冥邈、神逸方外，他的心境与大自然融为一体，反映了诗人摆脱世俗烦恼后的感受。"此中有真意，欲辨已忘言"指这里蕴含着人生的真正意义，想要分辨清楚却不知怎样表达。寓意从大自然的美景中领悟到了人生的意趣，指出辞官归隐乃是人生的真谛。

Wine-drinking Song

(V)

In people's haunt I build my cot,
Of wheel's and hoof's noise I hear not.
How can it leave on me no trace?
Secluded heart makes secluded place.
I pick chrysanthemums at will,
Carefree, I see the Southern Hill.
The mountain air is fresh day and night,
Together birds go home in flight.
What revelation at this view?
Words fail me if I try to tell you.

饮 酒
（二十首其七）

秋菊有佳色，裛①露掇其英②。
泛此忘忧物，远我遗世情。
一觞虽独进，杯尽壶自倾。
日入群动③息，归鸟趋林鸣。
啸傲东轩下，聊复得此生。

① 裛(yì)：通"浥"，沾湿。
② 英：花。

③ 群动：各种动物。

在百花早已凋谢的秋季，唯有菊花不为严霜粲然独放，寓意着诗人志趣高洁。"泛此忘忧物，远我遗世情"指菊泡酒中味更美，避俗之情更深浓，表现了诗人处在优美环境中的乐趣、闲适的心情和不愿与世俗为伍的感想。"啸傲东轩下，聊复得此生"指歌咏自得于东窗下，姑且逍遥度此生，表现出诗人壮志难酬的憾恨，并非一味悠然陶然，实际蕴藏着深沉的感伤，亦表达了他隐居终生的决心。

Wine-drinking Song

(VII)

Lovely chrysanthemums have autumn hue,
I pluck their fresh petals impearled with dew.
Dew-sweetened wine would drive sorrow away.
How could worldly cares in my heart still stay!
Although I drink with no one by my side,
Wine pours out from the pot when cup is dried.
All the bustle sinks with the sinking sun,
Birds flying to the woods sing on the run.
Proudly I croon in eastern corridor,
Glad to find a nearly lost day once more.

饮　酒

（二十首其八）

青松在东园，众草没其姿。
凝霜殄①异类②，卓然见高枝。
连林人不觉，独树众乃奇。
提壶抚寒柯，远望时复为。
吾生梦幻间，何事绁③尘羁！

① 殄(tiǎn)：杀尽，灭尽。
② 异类：指杂草。
③ 绁(xiè)：牵绊。

"青松在东园，众草没其姿"说的是青翠的松树生长在东园里，荒草埋没了它的身姿，暗喻诗人当前的孤独。而"卓然见高枝"又表现青松凌寒挺立孤高的品格，意在做人应当像孤松一样，不应苟合于世俗，随波逐流。诗人喜爱这青松，便将酒壶挂在松枝之上，流连于松树之下，也常从远处来瞻望青松的卓然高节，以滋养自己的精神境界。"吾生梦幻间，何事继尘羁"指感叹自己这一生好像在梦幻里，岂能被尘俗的羁绊拘牵，寓意人生之短暂，生命之珍惜。

Wine-drinking Song

(VIII)

In eastern garden stands a pine-tree green,

Its beauty veiled by shrubs cannot be seen.

When other plants are withered in hoar frost,

We find its lofty branch which seems long lost.

No trees in the woods can attract the eye,

We marvel at the single pine so high.

I stroke its wintry bough, wine pot in hand,

And gaze afar, lost in the wonderland.

Life changes from lost illusion to vain dreams,

Why should be drowned in eventful streams?

饮 酒

(二十首其九)

清晨闻叩门,倒裳往自开。
问子为谁欤,田父有好怀[①]。
壶浆远见候,疑我与时乖[②]。
褴褛茅檐下,未足[③]为高栖。
一世皆尚同[④],愿君汩[⑤]其泥。
深感父老言,禀气寡所谐。
纡辔[⑥]诚可学,违己讵非迷?
且共欢此饮,吾驾不可回。

① 好怀:热心肠,好心肠。
② 乖:背离,违背。
③ 足:值得
④ 尚同:同流合污。
⑤ 汩:搅乱,弄混。
⑥ 纡(yū)辔(pèi):把车倒回去。

"清晨闻叩门,倒裳往自开"指清早就听到敲门声,来不及整理好衣服就去开门了,表现出是在自然而融洽的气氛中。"壶浆远见候"指提着酒壶远道来探望,意为善良的老农劝告诗人姑且与世人同沉浮,不要独清。"深感父老言,禀气寡所谐"指深深地感谢父老言,无奈天生不合群,只得委婉地拒绝,表现出诗人不愿违背自己的初衷而随世浮沉,并一再决心要保持高洁的志向、隐逸避世、远离尘俗。

Wine-drinking Song

(IX)

Hearing a knock at dawn while still at rest,
I got up to open, not yet half dressed.
Asking the early comer, "Who are you?"
I saw a smiling farmer come in view.
He came to see me with a pot of wine,
Doubting if worldly offer I'd decline.
"You live in rags under a thatched roof.
But how can your cottage be riches-proof?
Since all the world is drifting with the tide,
Could you alone stand aloft and aside?"
I thank the farmer for his kind advice,
But it's my freedom I won't sacrifice.
Though I may learn to go official way,
To do against my will, can I not stray?
Let us rejoice at drinking the cup dry!
I won't go backward as the days go by.

饮 酒

（二十首其十）

在昔曾远游，直至东海隅。
道路迥且长，风波阻中途。
此行谁使然？ 似为饥所驱。
倾身①营一饱，少许便有馀。　　　　　①倾身：竭尽全力。
恐此非名计，息驾归闲居。

"风波"有两层含义，一是水面上的风和波浪，二是官场的动荡、龌龊。"此行谁使然？似为饥所驱"指谁使我来作远游，似为饥饿所驱遣。诗人自问自答，诗人感到自己既不力求功名富贵，而如此劳心疲力，倒不如归隐闲居以保持纯洁的节操。"恐此非名计，息驾归闲居"指恐怕此行毁名誉，弃官归隐心悠闲，可以看出诗人归田之心的迫切，体现诗人坚持洁身自好之志。

Wine-drinking Song

(X)

In bygone days I traveled far and wide,
Nearly as far as the eastern seaside.
Can I forget my journey hard and long,
Impeded by heavy rain and wind strong?
For what should I have gone such a long way,
Were I not driven by hunger I'd stay?
I did my best to get my daily meal,
A little bit seemed to me a great deal.
Afraid no office work was worth my strife,
I would go back to live my rural life.

饮 酒

（二十首其十一）

颜生称为仁，荣公言有道。
屡空[①]不获年[②]，长饥至于老。
虽留身后名，一生亦枯槁。
死去何所知，称心固为好。
客[③]养千金躯，临化消其宝。
裸葬何必恶，人当解意表。

① 屡空：指颜回生活穷困。
② 年：长寿。
③ 客：人生如过客，引申为人生短暂。

"颜生称为仁，荣公言有道"指人称颜回是仁者，又说荣公有道心，而颜回穷困并且短命，荣公挨饿至终身，虽然留名百世，但一生却憔悴甚至清贫，死后什么也不知道了，应在生前称心自任。诗人通过对人生的思考，表达了其人生观与处世态度。诗人认为，那种为追求身后的名声而固穷守节、苦己身心的行为是不值得的；同样，那种为希望能得到长寿而认真保养贵体的行为也是不值得的。诗人主张人生当称心适意，不必有所顾忌，在当今时代亦不必有所追求。"人当解意表"指返归自然才是真，尽显真意。

Wine-drinking Song

(XI)

Yan* was wise in his day;
Rong* knew to go his way.
But Yan did not live long,
Rong was poor all along.
They had posthumous fame.
What's the use of vain name?
Did they know after death
How to enjoy their breath?
Value your body high!
It's no use when you die.
Better buried unclad,
If people felt less sad.

* Yan and Rong were disciples of Confucius.

饮 酒

（二十首其十三）

有客常同止，取舍邈异境。
一士常独醉，一夫终年醒。
醒醉还相笑，发言各不领。
规规一何①愚？兀傲②差③若颖。
寄言酣中客，日没烛当秉。

① 一何：多么。
② 兀傲：倔强，狂傲。
③ 差：比较。

"有客常同止，取舍邈异境"指两人常常在一起，志趣心境是不同的。所谓田园生活，饥寒是常事，这首诗以醉者同醒者打比方，表现两种迥然不同的人生态度。"醒醉还相笑，发言各不领"指醒了醉了，都只能与另一个自己相顾大笑。醒着的时候，世事纷然眼前，诗人对这样的世道是厌恶的；醉了的时候，猖狂自在，不拘礼教反倒可能让自己怡然自得些。在比较与评价中，诗人愿醉而不愿醒，以寄托对现实不满的激愤之情。

Wine-drinking Song

(XIII)

Two men who live under one and same roof
Go different ways apart and aloof.
A man of letters drunken would appear;
A man of arms stays sober all the year.
They talk and laugh each at the other's way
Of living and seem to laugh it away.
How foolish is a man laden with care!
How proud is the man who drinks in the air!
I would like to tell the drinker to light
A candle so as to drink in the night.

饮 酒

（二十首其十四）

故人赏我趣，挈壶相与至。
班荆①坐松下，数斟已复醉。　　　① 班荆：把荆条铺在地上。
父老杂乱言，觞酌失行次。
不觉知有我，安知物为贵？
悠悠②迷所留，酒中有深味。　　　② 悠悠：醉酒后迷迷糊糊的样子。

　　陶渊明在偏僻山村，没有世俗侵扰，时常醉酒之后反而诗兴大发，胡乱扯出一张纸，书写感慨，等到第二天清醒后，再修改润色。"故人赏我趣，挈壶相与至"指老友赏识我的志趣，相约携酒到一起。诗中显现的是乡间独有的纯朴之情，使人会意中到来的都是淳厚质朴之人。"不觉知有我，安知物为贵"指已经不觉世上有我在，身外之物又有什么可值得珍惜的，表现诗人醉酒中的忘我之境，有点人与自然融合的味道了。"酒中有深味"指诗人从酒中体味出深意，话有说完的时候但其意却无穷，表现了诗人高洁傲岸的道德情操和安贫乐道的生活情趣。

Wine-drinking Song

(XIV)

Old friends who know my love of wine
Come, bottle in hand, to see me.
We sit on bushes beneath the pine,
After a few rounds drunk are we.
All at once old men chat away;
Out of tune we pass round the cup.
We don't know who we are today.
Can we value what's down or up?
Long, long we are lost in the drink;
In the delight of wine we sink.

饮 酒

（二十首其十六）

少年罕人事，游好在六经①。
行行②向不惑③，淹留④遂无成。
竟⑤抱固穷节，饥寒饱所更⑥。
弊庐交悲风，荒草没前庭。
披褐守长夜，晨鸡不肯鸣。
孟公⑦不在兹，终以翳⑧吾情。

① 六经：即六种儒家经典，指《诗》《书》《易》《礼》《乐》《春秋》。这里泛指古代的经籍。
② 行行：一直走，比喻时间不停地流逝。
③ 不惑：四十岁。
④ 淹留：长时间停留，指退隐一事无成。
⑤ 竟：最后，最终。
⑥ 更：经历，经受。
⑦ 孟公：东汉刘龚，字孟公。皇甫谧《高士传》载："张仲蔚，平陵人。好诗赋，常居贫素，所处蓬蒿没人。时人莫识，惟刘龚知之。"陶渊明在这里是以张仲蔚自比，慨叹没有像刘龚那样的知音。
⑧ 翳：遮蔽，隐没。

"少年罕人事，游好在六经"指自小就很少有世俗上的交往，一心爱好六经，指出诗人少年时就颇有壮志。然而老年一事无成，一生抱定固穷之节，饱受饥寒之苦。"弊庐交悲风，荒草没前庭"指破旧茅屋风吹凄厉，荒草已经将前院掩没，尽显诗人凄凉悲伤之感。但在诗人看来这并不是最难过的。"孟公不在兹，终以翳吾情"指没有知音在身边，没有人可以听我倾诉衷情，这才是诗人最悲哀的事情。

Wine-drinking Song

(XVI)

While young, I had social relation cold,

And only indulged in six classics old.

Now I am nearly forty years of age,

But life does not turn for me a new page.

I did not fear all my life to be poor.

Could I suffer from hunger any more?

My wretched cottage hears grievous wind pass;

My front yard buried in weeds and grass.

I don my coat to stay the long, long night;

My cock won't crow to welcome morning light.

If ancient connoisseur Meng were near me,

To tell him what I feel I would be free.

饮 酒

（二十首其十七）

幽兰生前庭，含熏待清风。
清风脱然①至，见别萧艾中。
行行失故路，任道②或能通。
觉悟当念迁，鸟尽废良弓③。

① 脱然：轻快的样子。

② 任道：顺应自然。

③ 鸟尽废良弓：语出《史记·越王勾践世家》："蜚(fēi)(飞)鸟尽，良弓藏。"比喻统治者在自己成功后杀掉以前对自己有功的人。

"幽兰生前庭，含熏待清风"指兰花生长在前庭，含香等待着清风，意在诗人通过兰花来喻指君子的高贵品格，用清风比喻君子之德要有明君赏识，表达了自己内心对高洁品性的坚守。"见别萧艾中"指在杂草中香兰自分明，意在诗人将萧艾比喻无能小人，表达了君子要在明时出仕才会有所作为，才能从平庸之辈中脱颖而出，暗指自己有着清高芳洁的品性。"鸟尽废良弓"指诗人也从这个典故说明自己归隐的原因，意在希望自己在迷失的人生道路上能够觉悟，回到原来的地方去，蕴含深刻的政治含义。

Wine-drinking Song

(XVII)

Sweet orchid in the front yard grows,
With fragrance waiting for the breeze.
The welcome breeze rises and blows,
Sweeping the weeds breeding disease.
In life's journey I lost my way
Until I see a gleam of light.
I know I'd hide my bow and stay
At home when there's no bird in flight.

饮 酒
（二十首其十九）

畴昔苦长饥，投耒去学仕。
将养①不得节②，冻馁固缠己。
是时向立年③，志意多所耻。
遂尽介然分④，拂衣归田里。
冉冉⑤星气流⑥，亭亭⑦复一纪⑧。
世路廓悠悠，杨朱所以止。
虽无挥金事⑨，浊酒聊可恃。

① 将养：休息调养。
② 节：法度。
③ 向立：快要三十岁的时候。
④ 介然分：耿直的本分。
⑤ 冉冉：渐渐。
⑥ 星气流：星宿节气运行变化，指时光流逝。
⑦ 亭亭：时间非常久远。
⑧ 一纪：十二年。
⑨ 挥金事：《汉书·疏广传》载：汉宣帝时太子太傅疏广辞官归乡后，将皇帝赐予的黄金宴请宾朋，挥金无数。

"畴昔苦长饥，投耒去学仕"指昔日苦于饥饿，抛开农具去为官，意在指诗人在这期间虽因饥寒而出仕，内心却是不平静的，而归田后依然未能解决意识问题。"是时向立年，志意多所耻"指那时年近30岁，内心为之甚是羞惭，表现了归隐的志趣与对仕途的厌恶。"虽无挥金事，浊酒聊可恃"指虽无挥金乐，浊酒足慰我心田，表明诗人尽管目前的境遇同样贫困，但走的是正途，没有违背初衷，且有酒可以自慰，心里是十分满足的。

Wine-drinking Song

(XIX)

Underfed for long in my native land,
I left the hoe to take the pen in hand.
I had not enough to feed my household.
Could we not suffer from hunger and cold?
When I was nearly thirty years of age,
I felt ashamed to face the ancient sage.
Then I resolved to go my former way
To live a rural life to end my day.
Star on star breathes an air current high;
Year by year a dozen springs have gone by.
The way of the world is so wide and long,
Even a philosopher would go wrong.
Though I have no gold to provide a feast,
I may drink cups of home-made wine at least.

饮 酒
（二十首其二十）

羲农去我久，举世少复真。
汲汲①鲁中叟②，弥缝③使其淳。
凤鸟虽不至，礼乐暂得新。
洙泗④辍微响⑤，漂流⑥速狂秦。
诗书复何罪？一朝成灰尘。
区区诸老翁，为事诚殷勤。
如何绝世下，六籍⑦无一亲⑧。
终日驰车走，不见所问津。
若复不快饮，空负头上巾。
但恨多谬误，君当恕醉人。

① 汲汲：形容心情十分急切。
② 鲁中叟：孔子。
③ 弥缝：弥补过失。
④ 洙（zhū）泗（sì）：两条河流的名称，在今山东省曲阜县北，孔子曾在那里教授弟子。
⑤ 微响：微妙的言语。
⑥ 漂流：时间的流逝。
⑦ 六籍：指六经。
⑧ 亲：亲近。

"羲农去我久，举世少复真"指伏羲神农已遥远，世间已经少有朴真之人了。诗人感叹伏羲神农时代的淳朴风尚已遗失殆尽，通过对孔子时期的道德风尚和文化业绩的景仰之情，以及秦汉之际儒家学者对文化典籍的热情，暗喻对现实社会败坏的悲慨。"终日驰车走，不见所问津"指世人奔走多为名利，治世之道无人问津，意在斥责当时的无耻世风，也体现诗人伤感之情。"但恨多谬误，君当恕醉人"指只是遗憾说了多有得罪大家的谬误酒话，望君原谅我这喝醉的人。因为避免招致杀身之祸，只能说自己的观点多为"酒话"。

Wine-drinking Song

(XX)

Far, far away ancient emperors' days,
No one still lives in their natural ways.
Confucius taught disciples without rest
To purify the world from east to west.
Though the auspicious bird did not alight,
They tried still to renew music and rite.
But two River songs were not heard to sing,
The stream of time passed till the tyrant king,
Who ordered Books of Poetry should be burned
And no more classics should again be learned.
Only a few old scholars tried to spread
The six Confucian classics to be read.
Why then after the Han Dynasty's fall
Would no scholar study Six Books at all?
So many chariots run all the day long,
But nowhere is heard the sagacious song.
If I did not drink my fill, flee from care,
Could I be worthy of the hood I wear?
But I regret the mistakes I have made.
Would you forgive what a drunkard has said?

止 酒①

①止酒：戒酒。止：句末语气助词，无实意。

居止②次城邑，逍遥自闲止。

坐止高荫下，步止荜门里。

好味止园葵，大懽③止稚子。

平生不止酒，止酒情无喜。

暮止不安寝，晨止不能起。

日日欲止之，营卫④止不理。

徒知止不乐，未知止利己。

始觉止为善，今朝真止矣。

从此一止去，将止扶桑⑤涘。

清颜止宿容，奚止千万祀⑥！

②居止：居住。

③懽（huān）：同"欢"，快乐，欢乐。

④营卫：中医上的气血和免疫功能。

⑤扶桑：中国古人认为这是太阳出来的地方。

⑥祀：年。

公元402年，陶渊明38岁，为其闲居时所作。这时的诗人居住在上京（晋江西九江市郊）老家，家境上有略见有裕的基础，也有可能是家人再三劝告其戒酒，诗人也决心戒酒，便有了此诗。全诗每句话都有一"止"字，读起来风趣盎然极具民歌情调，这也是诗人写作的一个特色。"平生不止酒，止酒情无喜"指平生不肯停止饮酒，停止饮酒就会心里闷烦。表明诗人确实喜欢喝酒，这也是诗人一生中最大的嗜好，可以辞官，可以守穷，但不可一日无酒。体现出戒酒对诗人来说会是一件痛苦的事情。"清颜止宿容"指仙颜代替旧日的容貌，说明自己对于酒的依恋和将要戒酒的打算。

Abstinence

Living within the city bound,
I pass my days freely at leisure.
I take a seat on shady ground,
Or stroll within the gate with pleasure.
I only eat my herbage fine
And enjoy playing with my son.
I never abstrain from drinking wine;
Without wine, life is joyless one.
At night in bed I can't well stay;
Nor can I rise with rising sun.
If I abstain from day to day,
No harm to my health will be done.
I knew that unhappy I'd feel,
But not what good is done to me.
Now I know abstinence brings weal,
I will abstain today with glee.
If I could abstain as I'm told
Until I reach celestial spheres,
A young look would replace the old
And youth might last a thousand years.

责 子

白发被两鬓,肌肤不复实。

虽有五男儿,总不好纸笔。

阿舒已二八,懒惰故①无匹。

阿宣行②志学③,而不爱文术。

雍端年十三,不识六与七。

通子垂④九龄,但觅梨与栗。

天运苟如此,且进杯中物。

① 故:同"固",向来,一直。

② 行:行将,接近,将要。

③ 志学:十五岁。

④ 垂:接近。

这首诗大约作于公元408年,当时陶渊明44岁。这首诗有两位大诗人有着不同的看法,杜甫认为此诗是在批评儿子不求上进,而黄庭坚予以否认。细味此诗并联系其他作品,诗中确实有对诸子责备的意思,诗人另有《命子》及《与子俨等疏》,诗人对自己的儿子们为学、为人是有着严格要求的。诗人虽弃绝仕途,但对子女成器与否也是很关心的。"白发被两鬓,肌肤不复实",此句中,诗人指出自己有些老了,欲引下言。"虽有五男儿,总不好纸笔"指身边虽有五个男儿,却总不喜欢纸与笔。说明诗人对这五个儿子的文学有较大期望。怎奈几个儿子好像对此都不感兴趣,文中体现出那种又好气、又好笑的心情。诗人这是带着笑意的批评,亦是老人的舐犊情深。

Blaming Sons

My temples covered with white hair,
My skin wrinkled, my muscles slack.
Though I have five sons, none would care
To read or write in white or black.
My eldest son is now twice eight,
But lazy as him none appears.
My second son won't dedicate
Himself to arts at fifteen years.
My third and fourth sons at thirteen
Know not how much makes six plus seven.
My youngest son has nine years green;
'Mid pears and nuts he is in heaven.
If such be the decree divine,
What can I do but drink my wine?

拟 古

(九首其三)

仲春遘^①时雨,始雷发东隅。　　① 遘(gòu):遇上,遇见。

众蛰各潜骇,草木纵横舒。

翩翩新来燕,双双入我庐。

先巢故尚在,相将还旧居。

自从分别来,门庭日荒芜。

我心固匪石,君情定何如?

    公元 421 年,陶渊明 57 岁。那时离刘裕废晋恭帝司马德文不久,诗人虽隐居多年,但对晋恭帝被废以及晋王朝覆灭心存痛惜和哀惋之情。这组诗共 9 首,多为忧国忧时、寄托感慨之作,多有托古讽今之词。

    "仲春遘时雨,始雷发东隅"指二月喜逢春时雨,春雷阵阵发东边。说明新的一年又开始了,以描写季节的变化,草木自由生长、春燕返旧巢,表现诗人不因贫穷而改变隐居的志向,同时也暗喻对晋室为刘宋所取代而产生的愤慨。"我心固匪石,君情定何如"指我心坚定不改变,君意未知将何如,喻指诗人故国之思的信念坚定,不可动摇,蕴藏着一种极严肃的人生态度,极坚卓的品节。

Old Styled Verse

(III)

A happy rain in good time falls;
The first thunder from the east rolls.
Worms are awakened in mid-spring;
Grasses and plants begin to grow.
Swallows coming back wing to wing
Reenter my hut two by two.
"Your old nest is still on the beam
Where you may renew your dream.
Since you parted with me last year,
My yard lies waste now and again.
My heart is firm as rocks appear.
Do you feel the same now and then?"

拟 古

（九首其四）

迢迢①百尺楼，分明望四荒。
暮作归云宅，朝为飞鸟堂。
山河满目中，平原独茫茫。
古时功名士，慷慨争此场。
一旦百岁后，相与还北邙②。
松柏为人伐，高坟互低昂。
颓基无遗主③，游魂在何方？
荣华诚足贵，亦复可怜伤！

① 迢迢：本意是遥远的，这里形容楼台很高。

② 北邙：位于洛阳北面，东汉、魏、西晋的君臣很多埋葬于此，这里泛指坟墓。

③ 遗主：死者的后人。

这首诗写由登楼远眺而引起的对历史人生的感慨。"迢迢百尺楼，分明望四荒"指登上高高百尺楼，清晰可见远处四方。登楼之事，未必实有，而只是虚构形象，诗人借以抒发情怀。江山满目，茫茫无限。"古时功名士，慷慨争此场"指古时追逐功名利禄之人，慷慨追逐在山河、平原。功名士想到死后的冷落，诗人不禁感慨功名士其可怜可悲，历史沧桑，古今之变，尤显人生一世，何其短暂！抒发了诗人不慕荣华富贵、坚持隐居守节的志向与情怀。诗人否定功名富贵，就是对自己归田躬耕生活道路的肯定。

Old Styled Verse

(IV)

The hundred-foot-high tower proud

Commands superb views far and nigh.

At dusk it's crowned with drowsy cloud,

At dawn around it birds will fly.

Mountain on mountain, stream on stream,

All come in sight with boundless plain.

Heroes of yore with smile would beam

To win victory and glory vain.

They would die in a hundred years

And lie buried then underground.

Cypress or pine felled disappears,

Lofty tomb leveled down to mound.

A fallen empire has no heir,

Where could the roaming soul be found?

Glory is a castle in the air;

There is no hero but death-bound!

拟 古

（九首其七）

日暮天无云，春风扇微和。

佳人美①清夜，达曙②酣且歌。

歌竟长叹息，持此感人多。

皎皎云间月，灼灼叶中华③。

岂无一时好，不久当如何？

① 美：形容词用作动词，喜欢，喜爱。

② 达曙：一直到早上。

③ 华：同"花"。

全诗的情感有先乐后哀的明显转变，诗人的心情会因时、因地、因境而变化，感叹欢娱夜短、韶华易逝的悲哀，表现了诗人自伤迟暮的情绪。"日暮天无云，春风扇微和"指日暮长天无纤云，春风微送气温和。佳人对如此的良辰美景，自然激发了她的生活热情，激发了她对美好人生的热爱及对未来的憧憬。"歌竟长太息，持此感人多"一句中，诗人感叹好景不长、青春易逝的悲哀，以景抒情由乐转悲。"岂无一时好，不久当如何"指虽有一时风景好，好景不长当奈何！说明诗人也不免自伤暮年之至，同时显现了作者对人生的执着。

Old Styled Verse

(VII)

There is no cloud in evening sky;
The vernal wind has warmed the eye.
A songstress loves the tranquil night;
She drinks and sings till first daylight.
As night is soon replaced by morrow.
How can the fair not sigh with sorrow?
The moon looks brighter amid cloud;
The flower among leaves seems proud.
Every beauty has her day,
But how soon will it pass away!

拟 古

（九首其九）

种桑长江边，三年望当采。

枝条始欲茂，忽值山河改。

柯叶自摧折，根株浮沧海。

春蚕既无食，寒衣欲谁待^①？　　　① 待：依靠。

本不植高原，今日复何悔！

　　公元418年刘裕扶持晋恭帝登基，隔年又逼晋恭帝退位，改晋为宋。有人认为这首诗暗喻晋亡的一段历史。"种桑长江边，三年望当采"指种植桑树在江边，指望三年叶就可采摘。诗人以桑喻晋，寓意晋恭帝既已继位三年，应当做出些成绩。"忽值山河改"指忽然遇到山河更改，喻指刘宋更替司马氏晋朝。"本不植高原，今日复何悔"指桑树本应植根于高原，却被种在长江边，自取毁灭，现在后悔又有何用，暗喻晋室依赖于刘裕，今日又亡于刘裕，又如何可以追悔。诗人对于晋亡，沉痛至深，说明诗人绝非是忘世之人，他对于世道政治，仍然抱有坚定的是非判断和鲜明的爱憎之情。

Old Styled Verse

(IX)

Mulberries plant'd along the River Long,
Their leaves'll be gathered in three years in throng.
Maybe when boughs and twigs begin to sprout,
Suddenly flood from the mountains break out.
Branches and leaves would be torn from the trees,
Even trunks and roots might float to the seas.
The vernal Silkworms have no leaves to eat.
What could warm up your body, hands and feet?
With mulberries planted in places high,
When flood comes, you need not regret and sigh.

杂 诗

(八首其一)

人生无根蒂,飘如陌上尘。
分散逐风转,此已非常身①。
落地为兄弟,何必骨肉亲!
得欢当作乐,斗酒聚比邻。
盛年不重来,一日难再晨。
及时②当勉励,岁月不待人。

① 非常身:不是永恒的身体,即不是盛壮年之身。

② 及时:趁着年轻的时候。

本诗作于公元 414 年,陶渊明 50 岁,距其辞官归田已有 8 年。因时代思潮和家庭环境的影响,使陶渊明接受了儒家和道家两种不同的思想,培养了"猛志逸四海"和"性本爱丘山"的两种不同的志趣。

"人生无根蒂,飘如陌上尘"是说人生在世没有根蒂,漂泊如路上的尘土。诗人感叹人生命运不可把握,不免使人有些伤感。"斗酒聚比邻"是说遇到高兴的事就应当作乐,有酒就要邀请近邻共饮。诗人不同于寻常之人屈服于世事,而是执着地在生活中追求温暖的朋友之爱,并崇尚快乐。"及时当勉励,岁月不待人"是说应当趁年富力强之时勉励自己,光阴流逝不等人,诗人以此来警示世人。

Miscellaneous Poems

(I)

A man is rootless in his day,

Floating like dust along the way.

Blown east and west, no longer am I

Still the same as in days gone by.

When born, I may be called your brother,

Why then should we not love each other?

Let us enjoy when days are fine,

Call neighbors out to drink our wine!

The prime of our life won't come twice;

Each day can't have two mornings nice.

I urge you to rise with the sun,

For time and tide will wait for none.

杂 诗

（八首其二）

白日沦①西阿，素月出东岭。
遥遥万里辉，荡荡空中景②。
风来入房户，夜中枕席冷。
气变悟时易，不眠知夕永。
欲言无予和，挥杯劝孤影。
日月掷人去，有志不获骋③。
念此怀悲凄，终晓不能静。

① 沦：落，即照在，映在。

② 遥遥万里辉，荡荡空中景：月色铺满大地，广阔的天空上明月高悬。万里辉：指月光。荡荡：宽阔，广阔。景：同影，指月亮。

③ 骋：驰骋，指宏伟大志无法实现，自己的才能无法施展。

    这首诗写诗人长夜不眠的情怀，抒发了对事业无成的感慨。通过写秋夜之景展现凄凉的感思。

    开篇描写了日月更迭，万里辉煌的景象。"气变悟时易，不眠知夕永"是说风冷才知道节气变了，因为失眠而知道长夜的永恒。诗人因为天气的变换觉察出四时更替，衬托出凄寒心境。后面道出不眠的原因是没有能够陪自己说话喝酒的知己，从而感叹时光飞逝。"有志不获骋"是说有壮志却不能得到施展。正是诗人孤独苦闷、心怀悲凄的原因所在。想到自己坎坷的命途，悲凄之感直到天亮的时候都不能平静下来。全诗都充满了诗人对人生的叹息。

Miscellaneous Poems

(II)

Beyond the western hills sinks the sun white;

Over east ridge the moon sheds her pure light.

For miles and miles overflow the moonbeams;

The air is permeated with shadows and dreams.

With the west wind my lonely room is filled;

At dead of night my mat and pillow chilled.

In autumn's breath I hear seasonal song;

On sleepless bed I feel the night so long.

I want to talk, but to whom to confide?

I drink to lonely shadow by my side.

The sun and the moon rise and fall with speed,

But where can I gallop at will my steed?

Thinking of this, I am so much depressed.

How could my mind all the night long find rest!

杂 诗
（八首其三）

荣华难久居，盛衰不可量。
昔为三春蕖，今作秋莲房。
严霜结野草，枯悴未遽①央。　　①遽(jù)央：结束，引申为凋零。
日月有还周，我去不再阳。
眷眷②往昔时，忆此断人肠。　　②眷眷：依依不舍的样子，回头看。

"荣华难久居，盛衰不可量"指荣华难以长久停留，盛与衰也难以预料。暗示生命盛衰中皆有时间的存在；物壮必老，体现老庄的哲学及生命自然的规律。"日月还复周，我去不再阳"指日月周而复始野草又会复生，而我则一旦死去就不能再重生于这个世上。观察大自然并与自然界对话，体悟到人生易逝的道理，不免有些悲哀。"眷眷往昔时，忆此断人肠"指眷恋着先前的种种，再想到这些真让人断肠。意在说自己老了而感到悲伤，越发地眷念青春时代的美好时光。

Miscellaneous Poems

(III)

Prosperity cannot last long;

Rise and fall alternate their song.

Lotus flowers bloom after spring,

But autumn will lotus seed bring.

When grass is bitten by hoar frost,

The lotus withers, though not lost.

Sun and moon set and again rise;

None can revive after he dies.

From olden memories awoken,

Oh, how could my mind not be broken!

杂 诗

（八首其四）

丈夫志四海，我愿不知老。
亲戚共一处，子孙还相保。
觞弦肆①朝日，樽中酒不燥。
缓带尽欢娱，起晚眠常早。
孰若当世时，冰炭②满怀抱。
百年归丘垄，用此空名道③！

① 肆：摆放，陈列。

② 冰炭：两不相容矛盾的事物，这里指名和利。

③ 道：同"导"，引导，引领。

"丈夫志四海，我愿不知老"是说丈夫有志在四海，我愿意不知道自己将是老年人，意指诗人志向远大但并没有所获，却到老年了。接着写到亲戚和睦相处、子孙孝敬相互爱护；琴与酒终日摆在面前，杯子里的酒也从来满着，意指诗人隐居安处的自得之乐。"孰若当世时，冰炭满怀抱"是说有谁像当今世上人，满怀名利若冰炭。寓意贪和求名是两种互相矛盾的，同时对那些贪利求名的人表示鄙视。最后体现诗人新自然说的思想。

Miscellaneous Poems

(IV)

A lofty man should benefit four seas,

But I'd enjoy till old a life of ease.

I'd have my kinsmen under the same roof,

And all my children safe and sound, harm-proof.

I croon and play my lute morning or night;

My wine cup never dried affords delight.

Freely I'd drink my fill with loose belt ties;

Early I'd go to bed and late to rise.

Can I be like those who would climb up higher,

Worried for gain and loss like ice and fire?

All will be buried in the grave in time.

Why should we care for glory, though sublime!

这首诗是诗人回忆自己少壮之时的宏伟志向和乐观情绪，充满勃勃的生机；但是随着时光的流逝，诗人感到不仅气力渐退、身体一日不如一日，而且昔日的猛志已经减退，内心充满许多忧虑。眼见光阴荏苒，却又一事无成，更使诗人感到无限忧伤和恐惧。

杂 诗

(八首其五)

忆我少壮时,无乐自欣豫。
猛志逸①四海②,骞翮③思远翥④。
荏苒⑤岁月颓⑥,此心稍已去。
值欢无复娱,每每多忧虑。
气力渐衰损,转觉日不如。
壑舟无须臾⑦,引我不得住。
前途当几许? 未知止泊处。
古人惜寸阴,念此使人惧。

① 逸:超越,超过。

② 四海:天下。

③ 骞(qiān)翮(hé):展翅翱翔。

④ 翥(zhù):飞翔。

⑤ 荏(rěn)苒(rǎn):慢慢地过去。

⑥ 颓:流走,逝去。

⑦ 须臾:片刻,一会儿。

"忆我少壮时,无乐自欣豫。"是说回忆自己年轻时虽没有遇上快乐的事情,但心里也会自然地充满欢喜。意指诗人少壮时积极向上的生命状态。"荏苒岁月颓,此心稍已去"是说随着时光流逝,那雄心壮志也渐渐离开自己,意指此时诗人的人生体验以及生命多了些忧患。"壑舟无须臾,引我不得住"意指自然在变化中,生命衰老也亦是如此。"未知止泊处"是说不知道生命的归宿在何处,意指诗人因志业未成而产生的隐忧,生命价值还没有实现。最后提出生命的价值就是在每寸光阴之中所实现的,诗人念到此处便觉警惧,说明诗人依然存有奋发之心。

Miscellaneous Poems

(V)

I still remember in my prime
I could be happy in sad time.
Over the four seas I aimed high;
Spreading my wing I dreamed to fly.
But youthful days passed and grew old,
My zeal for life as soon turned cold.
Delightful things were not enjoyed;
Worries and cares often annoyed.
I feel my youthful strength no more,
Each day not as the day before.
Time like a stream will pass away;
And leads me on without delay.
How far ahead should I still float?
I know not where to moor my boat.
The ancients had no time to waste.
How can late-comers make no haste?

杂　诗

（八首其六）

昔闻长者言，掩耳每不喜。
奈何五十年，忽已亲此事。
求我盛年欢，一毫无复意。
去去①转欲速，此生岂再值！
倾家持作乐，竟②此岁月驶。
有子不留金③，何用身后置④！

① 去去：时光流逝。
② 竟：了结，结束。
③ 有子不留金：《汉书·疏广传》载：疏广官至太傅，后辞官归故里，挥金如土宴请宾朋，别人劝他留些钱为子孙置田产，他说："吾岂老悖不念子孙哉！顾自有旧田庐，令子孙勤力其中，足以供衣食，与凡人齐。今复增益之以为赢余，但教子孙怠堕耳。贤而多财，则损其志；愚而多财，则益其过。且夫富者，众人之怨也；吾既亡以教化子孙，不欲益其过而生怨。"
④ 置：置办，经营。

　　这首诗以盛年之欢同眼下状况相比较，深感岁月不饶人，且所剩时光不多，此生难再，当及时行乐。"昔闻长者言，掩耳每不喜"是说以前听老人回忆往事，常常不喜欢听将耳朵捂起来，意指小时候无忧无虑不会考虑到人生易老。下面写到诗人50岁的时候，亲自将此事经历一番，真切地感受到昔日长者们说的人生易老、亲故凋零的无奈。然而光阴匆匆再也没有当年那样欢乐的心境了；转而诗人又呈现豁达心境。"有子不留金，何用身后置"是说没有为子孙留下金钱，就更不必为自己死后再去经营了，意指留财不如留德，同时诗人感到自己时日无多了，此生可能难再追求及时行乐的生活了，亦表达了诗人坦然的心境。

Miscellaneous Poems

(VI)

When elders talked of bygone years,
Displeased, I would shut up my ears.
But fifty years have gone by now,
And time writes wrinkles on my brow.
I would recall youthful delight,
But I can find no pleasure slight.
Far, far away are bygone days.
Could I relive in olden ways?
To drink my fill I'd spare no gold;
I would keep pace with days grown old.
I'd leave no money for my sons;
There's no need if they're worthy ones.

杂 诗

(八首其七)

日月不肯迟，四时相催迫。
寒风拂枯条，落叶掩长陌。
弱质与运颓，玄鬓早已白。
素标插人头，前绗渐就窄。
家为逆①旅舍，我如当去客。
去去欲何之？南山有旧宅②。

① 逆：欢迎。
② 旧宅：祖宗的坟墓。

这首诗写的是诗人自叹衰老，虽行将就木，然而诗人却能以视死如归的态度对待人生，表现出其不喜不惧的达观境界。"日月不肯迟，四时相催迫"是说日月如梭从不缓慢，四季互相催促从不停步。诗人感叹时光飞逝。"弱质与运颓，玄鬓早已白"是说体质在减损消耗，而黑发也已变成满头的白发，诗人是在说自己的身体和志向都不佳，话中尽显伤感之情。"去去欲何之？南山有旧宅"是说前行将要去何方，南山（庐山）陶氏的墓地。意指诗人道出了死后的去处，落叶归根、永归于本宅陶氏墓地。

Miscellaneous Poems

(VII)

The sun and moon will not slow doom;

Four seasons press each other on.

The chilly wind strips trees away;

Fallen leaves strewn along the way.

My health turns weak with worsened fate;

My black hair has whitened of late.

Of age my head bears the pale sign,

My forward way on the decline.

My home becomes an inn for rest;

The dweller's rather like a guest.

Oh, where, oh, where can I still go?

To the graveyard 'neath southern hill.

杂 诗
（八首其八）

代耕本非望，所业在田桑。

躬耕未曾替，寒馁常糟糠。

岂期过满腹，但愿饱粳粮。

御冬足大布，粗絺①以应阳。　　　　　① 粗絺（chī）：粗糙的葛布。

正尔不能得，哀哉亦可伤！

人皆尽获宜，拙生失其方。

理也可奈何，且为陶一觞。

　　这首诗中，诗人自言努力躬耕，却常常饥寒交迫，只能依靠糟糠充饥、粗布御寒，勉强度日。顾念自身如此勤苦，而他人皆有所得，于理实在不通。无可奈何，只有借酒浇愁抚慰内心的愤愤不平。"代耕本非望，所业在田桑"是做官食俸禄非我所愿，耕种田地、植桑养蚕才是本行，意指诗人对当时仕途的厌恶，以及归田的决心。接下来写到诗人亲自参加农业劳动且未曾停止，因饥寒常吃粗劣的食物，说明诗人不善耕种。"但愿饱粳粮"是说但愿饱食吃细粮。意指诗人当前窘困的生活使其无奈且充满哀伤。"且为陶一觞"是说还是举杯痛饮将忧愁忘记吧，意指诗人即使饥寒交迫也不愿出仕，体现诗人孤傲高洁的品质及达观的心态。

Miscellaneous Poems

(VIII)

I do not hope to earn good wages;
To do farm work is all my due.
My folks have tilled the field for ages;
Hunger and cold are nothing new.
I never ask more than enough,
Satisfied with chaff and plain food,
Clad in winter clothes of poor stuff
And in summer garment not so good.
I cannot meet my humble need.
How sad to say with broken heart!
Others may thrive in word or deed,
I can't earn a living apart.
What can I do and how can I
Drown my grief but drink my cup dry!

咏贫士

（七首其一）

万族①各有托，孤云独无依。
暧暧②空中灭，何时见馀晖。
朝霞开宿雾，众鸟相与飞。
迟迟出林翮③，未夕复来归。
量力守故辙，岂不寒与饥？
知音苟不存，已矣何所悲。

① 万族：世间万物。族：类。

② 暧暧：昏昏暗暗的样子。

③ 翮（hé）：指鸟类翅膀。

该首诗通过对古代贫士的歌咏，表现了诗人安贫守志、不慕名利的情怀。诗旨在最后4句的抒情，而可堪玩味的是前两层的景语。"万族各有托，孤云独无依"指万物各自都有依靠，高洁的贫士漂泊孤独没有依靠。诗人自喻为高洁的贫士，象征着诗人孤独无依的处境和命运。"众鸟相与飞"指众鸟匆匆结伴飞，暗喻众多趋炎附势之人依附新宋政权。"知音苟不存，已矣何所悲"指既然世上无知音，在贫困中终此一生，也没有什么可悲伤的，表现出诗人守志不阿的高洁志趣。

A Poor Scholar

(I)

Every thing has its resting place;
Alone the cloud's drifting in vain.
Melting in air, it leaves no trace.
When can we see its glow again?
Morning clouds rise from mist of night,
All birds fly to welcome the day.
One in the woods is late in flight
But early on its homeward way.
I'll keep to beaten track of yore,
Though from hunger and thirst not free.
There're no connoisseurs any more.
Why should poverty sadden me?

读《山海经》

（十三首其一）

孟夏①草木长，绕屋树扶疏。

众鸟欣有托，吾亦爱吾庐。

既耕亦已种，时还读我书。

穷巷隔深辙，颇回故人车。

欢言酌春酒，摘我园中蔬。

微雨从东来，好风与之俱。

泛览《周王传》②，流观《山海》图。

俯仰终宇宙，不乐复何如？

① 孟夏：初夏。古人以孟、仲、季来划四季中每个季节的三个月，孟为第一，仲为第二，季为第三。

②《周王传》：又称《穆天子传》，是一部记载周穆王西游的书。

这是陶渊明隐居时所写读《山海经》十三首组诗中的第一首。此诗看似描写信手拈来的生活实况，其实质寓意深远，诗人胸中流出的是一首囊括宇宙境界的生命赞歌。开头写初夏之际，草木茂盛。"众鸟欣有托，吾亦爱吾庐"指众鸟快乐得好像有所寄托，我也喜爱我的茅庐。暗喻诗人是非常喜欢安雅清闲、自然平和的生活，体现出世间万物、包括诗人自身各得其所。诗人自耕自足，没有后顾之忧，也不会为五斗米而折腰，闲暇之余在书本中吮吸精神食粮。"微雨从东来，好风与之俱"指细雨从东方而来，夹杂着清爽的风。寓意这样的人生快乐，在昏昏然的官场上是无法得到的。体现了诗人高远旷达的人生境界。

Reading *The Book of Mountains and Seas*

(I)

In early summer plants and grass grow high;
Around my cottage trees cast leafy shade.
Here birds rejoice to sing their lullaby,
So I love my thatched hut in the glade.
After I've tilled the land and sown the seed,
I may come back to read my books at leisure.
My lane's too humble for carriage and steed,
Where visitors can't find any more pleasure.
Still I am happy to drink my spring wine,
And pluck from my garden the herbage green.
A fine rain from the east tries to combine
With a fair breeze to beautify the scene.
I read *The Myth of Legendary King*
And *The Book with Maps of Mountains and Seas*.
I see the ups and downs from spring to spring.
What is happier than to do what I please?

拟挽歌辞

（三首其一）

有生必有死，早终非命促。
昨暮同为人，今旦在鬼录。
魂气散何之？枯形寄空木。
娇儿索①父啼，良友抚我哭。　　　①索：寻找。
得失不复知，是非安能觉？
千秋万岁后，谁知荣与辱。
但恨在世时，饮酒不得足。

陶渊明一生究竟是只活了五十几岁，还是活到63岁，至今都有争议，因此这一组自挽的诗是否是诗人临终前绝笔也就有了分歧。"有生必有死，早终非命促"指人有生必有死，即使死得早也不算短命。这一句体现诗人对生死观的中心思想，虽看似平淡却实有至理。"得失不复知，是非安能觉"，死去就不知道得与失了，哪还会有是非之感？诗人对人生的感悟是人死后一了百了，再无知觉，不如在世的时候多喝几杯酒，体现出诗人旷达的人生态度。"但恨在世时，饮酒不得足"指只恨今生在世时，饮酒不足太遗憾，最后以幽默诙谐的诗句写出肺腑之言。

An Elegy for Myself

(I)

Where there is life, there must be death;
In due time we'll breathe our last breath.
Last night we lived and filled our posts;
Today my name's among the ghosts.
Where is my soul fled far away?
But shriveled forms in coffin stay.
My children miss their father, crying;
My friends caress my body, sighing.
For gain or loss I no more care;
Right or wrong is not my affair.
Thousands of years will pass away,
And shame and glory of today.
But I regret, while living still,
I have not drunk wine to my fill.

图书在版编目（CIP）数据

许渊冲译陶渊明诗选：汉文，英文 /（东晋）陶渊明著；许渊冲编译 . -- 北京：中译出版社，2021.1（2022.7 重印）
（许渊冲英译作品）
ISBN 978-7-5001-6456-2

Ⅰ. ①许… Ⅱ. ①陶… ②许… Ⅲ. ①古典诗歌－诗集－中国－东晋时代－汉、英 Ⅳ. ①I222.737.2

中国版本图书馆 CIP 数据核字（2020）第 240381 号

出版发行	中译出版社
地　　址	北京市西城区新街口外大街28号普天德胜大厦主楼4层
电　　话	(010) 68359719
邮　　编	100088
电子邮箱	book@ctph.com.cn
网　　址	http://www.ctph.com.cn
出 版 人	乔卫兵
总 策 划	刘永淳
责任编辑	刘香玲　张　旭
文字编辑	王秋璎　张莞嘉　赵浠彤
营销编辑	毕竞方
赏　　析	代晓艺
封面制作	刘　哲
内文制作	黄　浩　北京竹页文化传媒有限公司
印　　刷	北京顶佳世纪印刷有限公司
经　　销	新华书店
规　　格	840mm×1092mm　1/32
印　　张	5.5
字　　数	110千
版　　次	2021年1月第1版
印　　次	2022年7月第4次

ISBN 978-7-5001-6456-2　定价：39.00元

版权所有　侵权必究
中译出版社